Whispers in the Wind

MARSHA ALEXANDER

MAJOR BOOKS • CANOGA PARK, CALIFORNIA

For my mother, Lee Durchin

MAJOR BOOKS
21335 Roscoe Boulevard
Canoga Park, California 91304

PRINTED IN THE UNITED STATES OF AMERICA

ISBN 0-89041-174-3

CHAPTER ONE

A SOFT RAIN FELL over the estate known as Bloodstone, misting its rococo turrets and the large baroque cupola whose tip, on even the clearest of days, seemed to pierce the sky. The penetrating moisture turned the trunks and limbs of feathery pine trees on either side of the house a deep cinnamon brown. The air was cloyingly scented with drenched vegetation, soaked firewood, and bleached rocks and boulders, freshly washed after months of baking under the hot summer sun.

Eleanor Lawrence stood motionless by the heavy velvet drapes in what was now her room. One slim hand parted the gossamer undercurtain as she stared through the leaded glass at the long-abandoned stables and the wilderness beyond. She cracked the window slightly, welcoming the damp air with its brisk outdoors fragrance. For the first time she allowed herself to wonder if she had done the right thing in coming to the remote mountain estate. . . .

The furrowed sky and the steady rain cast a gloom over the lush countryside, partially obscuring the awesome mountains with their bald domes and rugged peaks. Yet exquisite as the scenery was, she saw only the reflection of her own muddled and gray thoughts wherever she looked. An all-pervading sadness settled around her slight form like an invisible shroud, cooling her flesh in spite of the warmth of the room. *It's only the weather,* she told herself, shivering slightly. *Oh, if it were only the weather. Why do I feel as if something was terribly wrong? I never feel like this. . . . Only since I've come to this house. . . .*

Her duties as nurse to the baby daughter of Catherine and Michael Matthews had kept her active and distracted during her first three days at Bloodstone. Yet even then she had felt it, this odd depression. It was like a strange, unpleasant tugging from somewhere outside of herself, from the house itself, an inaudible wailing that she perceived through some unnamed sense organ in the very core of her being. And now it had managed to seep into her soul without her knowledge or permission . . . nibbling with insidious persistence at her fraying nerves since the sky had split open earlier that morning.

Eleanor gripped the silky curtain tightly, fighting the melancholia she felt with silent, tight-lipped determination. She felt weaponless and terribly vulnerable as the sensation of sadness and isolation grew. *How stupid! I can't imagine why I feel this way!* Her mind immediately touched on the

6

impending romance she had narrowly avoided by coming to Bloodstone. She had walked out on Dr. James Munroe to avoid the very emotions which were now threatening to overwhelm her. *Is that it? Is it Jim? But that doesn't make sense, not when I know I've done exactly the right thing!*

Her attempts at logic were wasted. They did nothing to dispatch her unhappiness. Each glistening drop of rain coaxed tears closer to the surface until they finally welled on the thickly lashed rims of her large brown eyes, breaking the light into a thousand dripping rainbows. *Enough! I give up. . . .* The hot wetness bathed her cheeks at once.

She stood quietly in the elaborately furnished room of the old victorian mansion and breathed in old perfume and the scent of decaying lace and dripping summer fern, while the rain ticked away in her ears like a clock moving at double time. Relaxing completely, she gave in to the poignant ache that had no name. The release felt surprisingly good, as if an overly taut spring somewhere inside her had been miraculously allowed to wind down.

She let the tears flow unchecked until the baby in the adjoining nursery cried out in its slumber. The kittenish mewing rose in volume, then melodically dipped back into silence before Eleanor could rouse herself from her damp musings. Dabbing with an ineffectual lace handkerchief, she walked quickly to the opened doorway between her quarters and the nursery, then carefully observed the tiny sleeper in the polished spool cradle. Feeling much better now that she had had her cry, Eleanor glanced over at the fire to make sure it was smokeless and steady. Without realizing it, her thoughts had shifted from herself to the infant.

Kierra Matthews was a beautiful child, with wisps of buttery yellow hair curling around a dimpled face that was both doll-like in its innocence and yet filled with an ageless wisdom. There was sadness in that tiny face also, as if she had already lived too long and seen too much.

"Poor darling," Eleanor said softly.

Kierra was what Eleanor and others in the medical world had come to call "environmentally retarded," a child that was not developing normally due to inadequate care, feeding, loving, or other outward conditions. She had begun life at a disadvantage, undersized and weak, giving evidence of physiological problems probably stemming from what Dr. Munroe had tentatively called alcoholic withdrawal, based on his knowledge of the mother's drinking problem throughout her pregnancy.

Jim had suggested the slim possibility that Kierra's condition could be the result of some form of brain damage instead, but Eleanor couldn't believe that. Although the baby had done poorly on every simple test the doctor could devise at his visit to the house, Eleanor was convinced that there was nothing wrong with the child other than sustained neglect. The infant had been dying from a lack of interest, a lack of love. The young nurse had no explanation for it, not in an environment such as Bloodstone, but all the indications were there, obvious even to the untrained eye.

The baby had been noticeably pale as if she had never been taken out of her room. She was painfully underweight, physically dirty, lethargic, and the frail body had been blistered with one of the worst cases of diaper rash Eleanor had ever seen. The young nurse had no idea how this could have happened with a mother, father, great-grandfather, and servants on hand. Kierra's father was a highly educated man, a historian who appeared to have sensitivity as well as intelligence. Eleanor knew that the baby's mother had earned a degree at an outstanding Eastern college. None of it made sense, and yet the facts were evident in the five-month-old infant. Kierra Matthews suffered from what Eleanor had previously thought of as the disease of poverty and the ghetto, where too many children, a lack of education, not enough money or time, was the usual culprit.

The baby's room bothered the nurse. Like her own, it gleamed from hours of careful labor and layers of polish applied meticulously by Teresa Sanchez, the Mexican housekeeper. Yet the nursery was somehow spartan, colorless and somber where it should have been bright and gay. Before Eleanor had come, the crib had been cornered by blank beige walls and a bland wood ceiling, with nothing to catch the curious eye of a resting baby. There were no toys, no dolls, no stuffed animals, such as abound in even the most modest of homes. To Eleanor, the nursery reflected the attitude of the entire family toward little Kierra. Most incredulous to the warmhearted nurse was that none of the Matthews had been to the nursery to visit the child once in the entire three days she had been there!

Her eyes touched on the mobile hanging over the cradle. She had bought it for Kierra the day she had come, a carnival of bright wooden animals in stripes and colors and riotous polka dots. It rocked slightly on its hanger, poised and waiting to spin out its tinkling music and fill the air with whirling reds and oranges, all designed to delight any infant.

Eleanor's lips curved in a soft, unconscious smile as she left the opened doorway and returned to her post at the window. Just that morning she had seen the light of dawning interest in Kierra's eyes as the mobile had spun for her. Already she anticipated her charge chortling like other babies her age. *I'll get you there, Kierra. I promise!* she thought with iron will, admitting to herself how important the baby's progress had already come to mean.

The incessant drumming of the rain brought the dark-haired young woman slowly back to herself, to her recent mood of doubtful reflection and sadness. But now she could think about it with a trace of dispassion, the tears having washed away the helplessness she had felt. *It really is the rain,* she thought more calmly. *The rain and possibly this house, too. This house! There's been tragedy here. I can feel it. It whispers its secrets from every wall. . . .* She turned her thoughts to her own problems and pains. *Even so, coming to Bloodstone was a good solution to what could have been a bad situation. Even Jim realizes that. . . .*

Her mind lingered on an image of Dr. James Munroe. The sudden quickening of her heart was a reminder that had she stayed on as the handsome young doctor's nurse much longer, she wouldn't have been able to resist his obvious attentions. She had been sharp enough to see the weakening in her defenses, the tendency to cast Jim's wife in the role of unsympathetic villain, his children as handcuffs from which he was powerless to escape. No, it was good she had taken this position, come to this strange and somehow mysterious house.

Thrusting aside all thoughts of her past employer, Eleanor made herself concentrate on the raw beauty of the land beyond the formally draped window of her new room. It was a chore made absurdly pleasant by the spectacular scenery everywhere. Her eyes feasted on barren cliffs, sloping mountains, waxy, green-leafed vegetation along with magnificent skies no amount of precipitation could dull. She contrasted this view against the dreary row upon row of parking lots and store fronts which had been her only vista during the two years she had worked in the ultramodern professional building in San Bernardino.

It already seemed very remote, as if she had been away from the city for a long, long time.

Eleanor found it impossible to identify herself with the girl she had been up until a handful of days ago. She had to strain to mentally recreate the neatly efficient young woman in the starched white nurse's dress moving through sharp-angled hallways, slim arms filled with charts. Her long brown hair had been rolled in a demure bun, her familiar face with its large round brown eyes, small nose, delicate mouth with the surprisingly full lower lip and sturdy, slightly clefted chin, all conventionally masked by powder, lipstick, eye shadow, and mascara. She thought of those eyes watering from daily smog abuse, and she had to smile. Although her growing up included a year in New York, six in Los Angeles, almost three in San Francisco, and one in Chicago, at heart she was a small-town girl.

It was strange how all those other years ran together in a disjointed way, like a Jackson Pollack painting, when the first ten years of her life were so crystal clear, preserved in her memory like a cherished jewel. She had lived in a rural community

11

in Pennsylvania, a little coal-mining area outside of Tamaqua called, aptly enough, Hometown. There she played in oak trees, ran across broad, grassy fields with her friends, sat before the big upright and tried to follow her piano teacher's instructions so that she, like her mother had done so many years before, could someday play at Carnegie Hall. It had been a simple, perfect life: one endless day in late spring, with ripe berries to nibble, games to play, secrets to share.

Then there was the accident in the mine, the nightmare of her father's funeral. A year of sadness passed in merciful haste, then her mother had met and married a traveling salesman who paid little attention to Eleanor, but locked horns with her older brother at once. Soon after they left Hometown and began moving from city to city, Richard got into trouble with the juvenile authorities. She had seen her brother only fleetingly from then on, and not at all since her mother's death two years before. They had never been close, however, and she rarely thought of him. She preferred to remember Richard as she did her parents and herself, picnicking in a meadow and holding buttercups under each other's chins. . . .

Eleanor let the curtain slip from her fingers, the soft, nostalgic smile still on her lips, feeling much better in spite of the ceaseless pattering of rain. Directly overhead, a squirrel scurried across the eaves, chattering noisily as it dodged raindrops that must have seemed as big as bullets. *It is nice being here.*

She walked to the huge mahogany dresser, her bare feet warm against the sumptuous Oriental rug with its fading design of painstakingly woven leaves and flowers. The room itself had a slight chill, though the fire laid by Ricardo, the housekeeper's son, was crackling in the hearth, spitting out a hearty warmth and a cheering brightness. In the broad mirror edged with hand-carved rose clusters over the dresser, Eleanor glanced at the reflection of the soundly sleeping baby, noting that the satiny comforter was still tucked snugly around Kierra's tiny shoulders. The entire house, she realized, had a definite air of dampness and a decisive chill that was never completely gone, not even on the warm days before this unexpected summer storm. Eleanor picked up a lacy white afghan intricately crocheted by some former Bloodstone wife or servant and draped it around her, crossing the edges generously over her small breasts.

Glancing up into the forgotten bureau mirror, she was momentarily startled to find herself gazing at a young woman who looked strangely out of focus with the world she had known before coming to this estate, but perfectly cast for her immediate setting. Disdaining the make-up she had only worn because it had been expected of her in the doctor's office, her unpainted eyes looked larger and younger than her twenty-three years, and her unlipsticked mouth had a softness and a naturally coral hue that no artificial coloring could duplicate. Her hair, almost to her small waist, hung loose and sable brown, waving softly around her face and outlining the lacy afghan and long muslin dress.

Something about the vision caused the breath to catch in her slender throat. It wasn't just that she looked unusually pretty, which she did—it was the timelessness of her appearance which had startled her. *Never have I looked so . . . so absolutely right,* she thought slowly. She touched the reassuring solidness of her oversized dresser while her eyes remained on her own image. *This house makes me feel like Alice . . . curiouser and curiouser. . . .* She had never before considered herself as a creature of any special time, though more than once she had felt strangely out of step with the world into which she had been born. Again she thought of the neatly garbed girl in the building of glass, stainless steel, and tastefully framed professional certificates on spotless white walls. She knew at once that this young woman with the loosely flowing hair and yellowing afghan was really her; that already the other *she* was fading beyond touch, a dress-up doll dancing to a broken record.

I belong here! she thought with very little surprise. The cool wood under her fingertips felt like polished glass as she traced the edge of the dresser and continued to stare at herself. *But why?* Eleanor began to wonder if she had come to Bloodstone simply to escape an attraction to a man she could not allow herself to love, or if something deeper and more compelling had brought her to the isolated estate buried high in the San Bernardino mountain range.

Never before had she thought of destiny in such a personal sense. And yet, with the rain hammering against the window, the tiny child asleep in the adjoining nursery, the image of herself as she might have looked in a world one hundred years gone, the young nurse knew she was precisely where she belonged. . . .

CHAPTER TWO

A SOFT TAPPING ON her door scattered her thoughts like shattered glass.

"Miss Lawrence?" The tapping increased in volume.

Eleanor hurried to the door, but the unmistakable stirrings from the nursery told her she hadn't been fast enough. A baby yawn was followed by a sleepy sniffle.

The Mexican housekeeper pressed a dark hand to a glossy knot of thick black hair streaked with gray. "Excuse me, please, nurse. Will you have dinner in your room again?" Her voice was lightly accented and very pleasant.

"Just a moment, Mrs. Sanchez. I have to get Kierra." She hurried into the other room and scooped up the baby. "Please come in, Mrs. Sanchez," she called through the opened doorway. "I won't be a second." She grinned at the yawning baby. "We're quick-change artists, aren't we?" After dropping the damp diaper into a nearby pail, Eleanor tested the bottle she had been warming on a hot plate she had requisitioned from the cavernous kitchen. Finally she carried the infant into the other room and settled into a small rocking chair.

Immediately she began to coax Kierra to take the bottle. "Come on now, sweetheart, you're hungry even if you don't know it." The baby's disinterest was as worrisome as ever, yet after a somewhat shortened period of urging, the nipple disappeared into Kierra's rosebud mouth. She hugged the baby a little more tightly, made sure that air bubbles were escaping through the warmed milk in a steady flow, then looked up at the housekeeper.

"I think she's beginning to get hungry in spite of herself. I've worked with a few babies like this before—in my training. Babies in institutions, primarily. They're fed so impatiently in some situations that they get to distrust the bottle. They don't dare expect too much from it. Some of them become greedy eaters, working furiously to get as much as they can in the time they're given. Others, like this poor baby, simply lose interest." Her voice was informative and natural, but Eleanor felt anger and frustration beneath the surface of her calm. "I wish I could get her to eat solid foods. Do you have a food mill in the kitchen? I'd like to try her on fresh apple and ripe banana. She won't have anything to do with cereal, but I don't suppose I'd care for it, either." Then, with little warning, the anger took over. "Poor little thing!" she said with irrepressible feeling.

The older woman glanced with a reluctant and passing interest at the infant, then turned to the nurse. "I will find whatever you require." Involuntarily her dark eyes returned to the baby. For a moment the rocklike face softened and a tiny click excaped her lips. Then the impassive expression settled back in place.

Eleanor contemplated the housekeeper silently. There was kindness and compassion on the woman's face, etched finely in lines of warmth and devotion. It struck Eleanor as unnatural that Mrs. Sanchez could be so aloof and distant to the mistreated child of a family to whom she appeared quite dedicated. Disturbed, she rocked the somberly nursing baby in her arms, feeling as protective as a lioness, as maternal as the Madonna. "Then I'd like the mill and the fruit for her dinner, please."

The woman nodded curtly. "I must get back to my work, miss. Will you have dinner in your room tonight? As usual?" she asked again, remembering why she had come. "Mr. Michael is returning from his trip to the city, and he asked if you would join him at dinner tonight. He would like a report on the progress of the child. I tell him you prefer to stay with the baby and I bring you a tray, but I promise to ask you."

Eleanor hesitated. There was so much about the family she wanted to know, and this would be her first opportunity to see them interact together. Yet she felt uncomfortable about being away from Kierra. Ricardo had offered to sit while she took her meals downstairs, but Eleanor felt uneasy at the thought of the baby being alone with anyone in the household until she had a better idea of who everyone really was. She was determined to see that nothing further happened to the child. More, she wanted Kierra to come to trust her to be there, at least until she discovered that the world could be a friendly place.

"Has Dr. Matthews been away?" It came as a mild shock to realize that she had been unconsciously looking for him during her walks with Kierra since the day she arrived. She had especially wondered why he had not been in to see his child since she had taken over.

The housekeeper bent gracefully from her slightly thickening waist and picked up a white thread from the dark rug. "He work on very important paper for the university. A grant. He go many times to Los Angeles and other places to do research." She nodded stiffly, but Eleanor could see the pride on her face, hear it in her melodic, faintly accented voice.

The young nurse couldn't help wondering if Teresa Sanchez felt as warmly disposed toward all members of the house. "I've been hoping to see more of Mrs. Matthews. I wanted to talk to her about the baby, but she seems to be very busy." Her cheeks pinked at the obviousness of her probing. "You did mention that I'd like a few words with her?"

The strong jaw set. "*Sí*. Of course."

The girl waited, but the housekeeper said nothing. Eleanor could feel the frost from where she sat. *Well, that takes care of mother and baby!*

"About dinner. . . . I think I'd better stay with Kierra. But tell Dr. Matthews I'll be happy to talk to him anytime."

The housekeeper nodded and started out the door. Then she hesitated.

The baby's mouth released the nipple and twisted into a grimace of discomfort, as if a full stomach were an unfamiliar and possibly unpleasant

18

phenomenon. "Yes?" Eleanor put down the bottle and brought the infant to her shoulder. Remembering the borrowed afghan, she hastily reached for a protective diaper from the freshly laundered stack she kept near the bed. From somewhere in the house a clock struck the hour.

Mrs. Sanchez turned around. "I . . . I want you to know that I ask to take care of the baby. When she was born. Mrs. Matthews, she refuse me. She was angry, she was very angry. She say she take care of the baby alone. But I offer." She looked hard at the diapered and sweatered infant, a glaze of unexpected tears over her sharp eyes. "It is not the baby's fault, what she is." Turning quickly, the woman left the room.

Automatically, Eleanor talked to the baby. "That's a good girl, such a good baby," she crooned absently, placing the full little stomach against her shoulder. She patted lightly, working the smooth warm palm of her hand over the supple little spine and the angel tips of Kierra's shoulder blades. She stared at the door which had closed silently behind Teresa Sanchez.

"It's not the baby's fault, what she is. . . ."

She kissed the silky-haired head. "What *are* you, sweetheart? *I* think you're a somber-faced angel who has to be taught to smile." She sighed. "Which certainly isn't your fault," she added, getting up and carrying the baby to the bed. She carefully peeled away the wet diaper and bathed and oiled the delicate skin, taking pains to be as gentle as she was thorough. She had spent the last three days in making sure that the infant was changed the instant she needed it, and already the flesh had lost its fiery redness and was responding to Eleanor's tender care. She pinned a spotless fluffy diaper in place, then pulled on a pair of knitted booties.

She walked into the nursery with the baby, her mind playing with the idea that Mrs. Sanchez had meant something else by her strange remark. By the crib she spread a lime-green baby blanket on the rug and placed Kierra on it, face up. Then she pulled the arm of the mobile so that it hung high over the baby and turned the key. Kierra looked up at the whirling animals and her tiny blonde eyebrows worked with a glimmering of interest.

Eleanor's checkered bag of crocheting was on a small table in the baby's room. She reached for it and sat down cross-legged on the floor next to her charge. "Isn't that pretty up there? And look at what I'm making for you here." She grinned at the baby who was still gazing expressionlessly at the mobile. Her hand dipped into the bag and lifted out a crochet hook and a loosely woven mass of sunny yellow yarn that was obviously well on its way to becoming a cuddly duck. She began to work the wool deftly over and under the hook, her thoughts returning to the baby and the oddness of Kierra's family. Eleanor was well aware of feeling an undeniable prejudice toward the Matthews. It had been born in her heart the moment she first laid eyes on the infant on her second visit to the house.

There had been no baby the first time she had come to Bloodstone. The old man, Lucas Matthews, had had a slight stroke in the middle of the night. Jim had recently become the family physician after the death of his father. "You might have to stay with Mr. Matthews," he had warned her over the phone. "But from the sound of it, I'm inclined to think it was a very mild stroke."

It had been a cold night, Eleanor remembered. "Why don't they have a doctor who lives closer?" They had been driving almost an hour from San Bernardino through twisting mountain roads lightly glazed with patches of black ice.

Jim had laughed. "Forest Falls is a very small town. I've heard that Bloodstone takes up most of it."

"Why is it called Bloodstone?"

He hadn't known. "Maybe it has some terrible past. Or maybe its former owners were Mr. and Mrs. Bloodstone." He grinned at her after negotiating a particularly tight curve. "That's one of the things I like about you, Eleanor. Your overly fertile, zany imagination."

She had been impressed with the sweeping beauty of the land beyond the huge cedars that marked the entrance to Bloodstone. The big mansion itself took her breath away. It was a dark, majestic structure of solid weathered beams, rock and stucco, with stained-glass windows, impenetrable turrets and the extravagant cupola which appeared to be lost in the star-packed sky overhead. It looked forbidding while somehow managing to maintain an equally dominant air of elegant welcome, but in so formal and frosty a manner that Eleanor was very glad she had come to Bloodstone for a definite purpose. Great twin gloves of yellow light illuminated the path and led to an impressive oak door that was studded with brass fittings and carved panels.

Where there had only been small dirty clumps of snow on the way up to the estate, there were now great shoulders of it on either side of the drive. As they pulled up to a parking site directly in front of the main entrance, Eleanor caught a glimpse of what appeared to be a natural sculpture behind the mansion, a small mountain of smooth boulders which clustered together uncomfortably close to the house. They looked like massive tonsured monks, but faceless, unreadable. In the vivid moonlight they looked strikingly sinister and grimly menacing, and their color was a deep, bloodlike crimson. She was about to point it out to Jim when the door opened and a young Mexican man quickly gestured them inside.

Eleanor finished her last stitch on the yellow duck's tail, then neatly tied her work and threaded the wool so that there would be no loose ends for the baby to unravel. The mobile was turning slowly now, and since Kierra still had her bright blue eyes on it, Eleanor wound the toy again, then darted into her bag for bits of colored yarn to fashion a face for her creation. "Won't be long now, sweetie." She let her mind return to her first exposure to Bloodstone, especially remembering Teresa Sanchez' concern for the old man.

After urging them inside, Ricardo had led them to Lucas' darkly elegant bedchamber. Michael, who had been up with his grandfather all night, had gone to his room for a few minutes. After a thorough examination, Jim had gone with Ricardo to speak to Michael, leaving her alone with Lucas Matthews and the housekeeper.

It had been obvious to Eleanor that the Mexican housekeeper was touchingly devoted to the old man. She had tended Lucas with the loving attentiveness of a deeply concerned friend or wife. Eleanor could reconstruct the woman's face in her mind, lined with worry and fear for the old man, pathetically eager to be of some help.

Her second visit to Bloodstone had been just four days earlier, yet Eleanor felt as if she knew the house—if not the occupants—intimately. The people seemed elusive to the girl, human fish who swam through a reality that seemed not to touch on hers at all. Eleanor had seen Catherine only once, when she came to Jim's office shortly before giving birth to Kierra. The nurse remembered her as being a startlingly beautiful redhead, obviously resentful of the pregnancy which had distorted her body. It had been plain that the woman had been drinking.

After the birth, Jim, greatly disgusted, had mentioned that Catherine had arrived at the hospital dead drunk, raining curses at him, her husband and Ricardo, who helped carry her to the waiting wheelchair. In white-lipped anger, Jim had called in Dr. Belote, the hospital pediatrician, for a closer look at the newborn. In dismissing mother and daughter three days later, he had left strict orders that Kierra be taken to Dr. Belote in a week so that her questionable condition could be carefully watched, and that Catherine herself return in six weeks for a postnatal checkup. When the redhead had not appeared for the examination, Jim had assumed that she must have found herself another doctor. But when Sy Belote mentioned that the baby hadn't been brought in once in the five months, he had grown concerned.

The housekeeper, with some confusion, had responded to Eleanor's phone call that Mrs. Matthews had mentioned taking the baby to Dr. Belote several times. An hour later, Dr. Matthews returned the call, requesting that Jim come to the estate to see the baby and asking to be recommended to a competent nurse to care for the infant.

Since Eleanor had trained in pediatrics, she offered to come along. She was curious about the baby's development after her poor start, and she admitted to herself that she was eager to see the elegant estate by daylight and in its summer dress. She was also interested to discover if the blood-red rocks behind the mansion were an illusion of the night or a product of what Jim called her overly fertile imagination.

But the house and its rich furnishings, the grounds with their showy summer foliage, even the cloistered rocks were completely forgotten when Eleanor looked at the baby lying so listlessly in the antique cradle. All she felt was fury and surprise.

She had seen cases like Kierra before. They languished in the homes of immature parents who had no time for the infants they had created in their careless passion. She had seen others, better cared for physically, but wearing the same blank expression of the neglected child, in understaffed institutions and orphanages. Pathetic babies, wasting away from lack of love and attention, babies no one really wanted, babies born with the sensitivity to know they were unwanted.

They conferred briefly. "I won't know for sure," Jim had said, "not until she's older. There could be some functional defect. . . ." But even then, looking into those baby eyes that seemed shadowed with resignation, Eleanor had felt sure that she knew, perhaps better than the doctor, what Kierra needed.

Catherine Matthews didn't appear at all, and Michael Matthews had taken Eleanor by surprise. She had not been prepared for the obvious concern and sincerity in those dark eyes, and the historian's quiet pain was no less than her own. He was tall and well built and looked more like an earnest and dedicated young M.D. in his dark suit than Jim did in his denim sports coat. He reminded her of Alan Alda, the actor, handsome in a clean-featured, sensitive way. Eleanor couldn't help but think him completely mismatched with his loud, cold, extravagantly beautiful wife.

"I had no idea," he had said softly after Dr. Munroe had sketched out a brief synopsis of Kierra's condition.

Jim had only touched on the baby's lack of motor and emotional development, softpedaling the possible retardation with well-chosen words and reassuring gestures. He barely skimmed the issue of the physical evidences of neglect.

"My God," Michael whispered, closing his eyes for a moment. "I should have known."

Oddly enough, Eleanor had believed him. She searched his pale serious face and got the distinct but surprising impression that Michael Matthews had had very little contact with his own child, that he was as startled by the baby's condition as she. Somehow that annoyed her more than if his had been a deliberate cruelty.

Her anger began to branch like the roots of a great tree—at Jim, for presenting the baby's case with a certain diffidence he would not have used with a less wealthy family; with this attractive and educated young father who could be oblivious to his own suffering infant; with herself, because she knew she was about to take the job as nurse to Kierra and blast herself from a dawning romance she should have had the strength to resist without having to run away like a child.

"How can it be," she heard herself asking from the depths of the pained frustration she felt, "that no one saw Kierra's condition before this? Why, among other things, that baby is suffering from malnutrition! In a house like this!"

Michael's eyes rested fully on hers, but he said nothing. They were dark and unreadable, but they didn't flinch beneath the harshness of her accusation.

Jim looked at her with barely concealed surprise, and he quickly began to speak. "Uh, often, in the case of a first child. . . ."

It was Michael who interrupted the doctor's attempt to rationalize on behalf of the family. "Please." He turned to Eleanor. "Do you think you could help my daughter?"

"I would like to try," she said simply, suddenly very sure that what she was doing would be best for everyone concerned. Her mind made up, she wanted to be in control of the baby as soon as possible. "Would it be all right if I left right away, Dr. Munroe? Judy and Shannon wouldn't have any trouble finding a replacement for me."

Jim gave his white-faced permission with a short nod.

It was not until they were seated in the doctor's snug Mercedes again that the dam had broken. Eleanor let Jim have his say, then reminded him of his commitments to his family.

"Don't think I'm going to forget you so easily, Ellie. You know that I've fallen in love with you."

Strangely, the words that had been unspoken between them—the words that a part of Eleanor had wanted to hear—left her unmoved. She had looked up at the handsome doctor and felt a wave of sadness. She thought of Jim's wife and his children, really thought of them, perhaps for the first time. However much she cared for Jim and he for her, he belonged to someone else. His talk of love bothered her now. Somehow it was like the neglected child she had just left, an ultimate unkindness, another cruelty in an already overburdened world. Had she ever imagined she, of all people, could build happiness on that?

Fumbling with words, she tried to explain. Jim hadn't understood. He had fought what he called her emotionalism with what he termed logic. But it was no good—something about that lethargic baby in the richly polished cradle had affected her deeply. It was important that she do something of value. She could help that poor infant. And she could get out of Jim's life.

Partly because she wanted to end the fruitless discussion, and also because she wanted to know as much about the Matthews as she could, Eleanor pumped Jim about them on their way down the hill.

"I really don't know much," he told her. "My father took care of the old man for years. He believed that Catherine Matthews, at twenty-six, was an incurable alcoholic. He tried to dry her out while she was pregnant, but she wasn't interested. You know the baby's birth condition. My own experience with Mrs. Matthews wasn't particularly pleasant. She's a spoiled, self-centered rich girl who thought it would be great fun to get married and install herself in a grand old mountain estate. Only she got bored. Fast. She never wanted the kid. I also gathered that she and old Mr. Matthews don't get along. My guess is that she's taken complete charge of the infant, which, God knows, is a pity. I don't know why—by the appearance of Kierra I'd say it's hardly been a labor of love. Maybe just to prove she can do it." He shook his head.

"You don't really think the baby has some sort of brain damage, do you?"

His light eyes had turned to her. "You know there's nothing definite in medicine. Every case is different. By judging the mother's history and the evidence of neglect, my guess is that the baby is only showing the beginning stages of withdrawal from an inhospitable world. I think she'd respond to positive treatment over a period of time. But that's only my guess. It's too soon to know for sure. In the meantime. . . ." He had given her terse, professional instructions about vitamins and diet, then fell into silence for the remainder of the trip home. There had been nothing else to say.

As if her fingers had a brain of their own, the yellow duck was finished and waiting to be stuffed. Eleanor smiled at the big blue eyes with their black-fringed eyelashes, the orange wool smile that crossed the white beak. She pulled clean but worn-out nylon stockings from her bag and began to stuff the toy. She grinned at the baby as the soft creature began to plump out and take on a lopsided, comical shape. "Now I never said it would look like a real duck." When it was filled enough, she deftly ran a stitch around the opened underbelly, tied it off, and pronounced the duck finished.

Excited as if she were the child with a new toy, Eleanor held the duck up for Kierra to see. "Isn't it silly, sweetheart? Don't you want to play with it? Come on, baby, reach for it. You can do it! Take it, sweetie, come on, that's my girl."

As if Kierra understood, one little hand twitched

and lifted slightly before falling back to the blanket. But the round eyes left the mobile and fastened onto the outlandish duck.

Eleanor placed the stuffed animal on the baby's chest, then tucked the little arm around it. "There!" That brought the duck's head right under Kierra's cheek. With comical sobriety, the baby wrinkled her brows and tried to focus on the yellow toy right under her nose. Her eyes crossed slightly, like a cat lining up its prey.

Laughing, Eleanor neatly balled her wool and put everything away. "Next you get a teddy bear and then we'll think about a clown or a baby doll. We'll fill this old room until it looks like a toy store. Boy, I can tell where my salary is going, already." She rearranged the duck so that the baby coud see it better. She stroked the pale yellow hair that was now like silk from the daily shampooings. "You sure are a pretty little girl, Kierra. Who do you look like? You don't have your daddy's dark hair. But I think you might turn out more like him someday. She recalled how Michael's eyes had held hers when she had accused him of indifference to his daughter's condition. She had felt a split-second of regret after she had spoken. His angular face with its intelligent eyes seemed so sensitive, so troubled, as if this outrage with Kierra was one more in a lifetime of unspeakable experiences, over which he had no control.

Eleanor had to smile at herself. *And I accused Jim of trying to save the genteel Matthews pride!* Yet it was not the same thing and she knew it. She had read something in his face, some hinted, non-verbal message she had not been able to decode, yet had understood on some deeper level. While she couldn't forgive his blindness, she could and did grudgingly admit to herself that something was happening at Bloodstone that she was not yet qualified to pass judgment upon. And there was something in Michael Matthews that kept her from passing judgment on him, as well.

Taking care not to dislodge the duck from its little mistress' arms, Eleanor picked her up. "Let's put on a warm playsuit and take you for a little walk around the house," she suggested, tickling the flat baby stomach. The rain had kept them in their rooms all day, and Eleanor felt a sudden desire for a change of scenery. She had managed to lose the oppressive sadness that had clung to her all morning, and she felt a relief that pleasantly restored her natural sense of well-being.

It wasn't until she had dressed Kierra in a bright pink playsuit that she found a word for Dr. Matthews which fully covered the feelings that had been aroused in her by the man. *He had seemed . . . tormented*, she thought with a small shock. Eleanor found the realization as perplexing as little Kierra's condition itself.

Once again the nurse had to smile at herself. Like all poor girls brought up in depressed coal towns, she naturally believed the myth that a great deal of wealth and comfort protected one from misery and despair. She thought of old Lucas as he had looked in his great bed on her first visit to Bloodstone, no different from other old men with pain who listened fearfully for the brush of death's wings nearby. Her mind skipped to Catherine, beautiful, young, rich— yet a deeply disturbed woman. The little baby she tended had been brought into a world of wealth, opportunity, and beauty, and her wasted body and unresponsive eyes were proof of her pitiable condition. She thought of the handsome historian and shuddered. She had come to a house of many secrets and much hidden pain. She picked up the baby and left the room.

The upstairs hallway was broad and self-consciously ornate, reminding Eleanor of Hollywood pomposity and old movie houses. She had loved the theaters more often than the pictures they had shown, slipping away from the images on the screen to bask in the quiet glory of the hallways and curving broad staircases. However noisy the movie, the thickly carpeted crimson floors and broad mahogany doors made the climb to the lounge an exciting, glamorous, and silent affair. She loved the paintings on the curving ceilings, the filigreed woodwork on the archways, the torchlike lighting fixtures which transported her to the days of Scheherazade in ways no costumed actress ever could.

This hallway at Bloodstone gave off the same timeless luxury and sense of grandiose privacy. She could almost smell the popcorn, salty and covered with hot golden butter. The wide pathway was complete with dark red carpets, the same thick walls ornamented with carved angels, shepherds, and cupids, brass lanterns throwing off a soft, indirect light day and night. Her door was farthest from the top of the grand stairway, with portals to the turrets and cupola as well as other bedroom doors opening on either side of the hallway. The top of the staircase was like a central room in itself, with a bay platform that overlooked the downstairs hallway. Large curved aquariums spanned either side of the bay, throwing light and a dreamy, underwater atmosphere over the steps and lower floor. Beyond the staircase were the other rooms and stairwells to another turret and two peaked upper rooms as well as the attic. Eleanor had counted the doors and knew there were twelve bedrooms, including the nursery and her own, but not including the servants' quarters on the main floor where Teresa Sanchez and her son each had a room.

She stopped in front of the large aquariums and let the baby inspect the iridescent fish in their watery world. She was about to point out the wriggling progress of a small turtle only to notice the infant's eyes fastened on the shelled creature. She held her quietly for several minutes until Kierra's interest flagged, then started down the stairs, her own mind lost in the delicious excitement of seeing the child of whom she had already become so fond begin to respond to her environment.

The total absence of sound as she descended the stairs made the clear, feminine voice near her sound startlingly loud. Eleanor stopped, then realized she was listening to a woman talking on the telephone in the library farther down the hall.

She continued on to the back of the staircase where the stroller was stored. It was one of several items she had requested on coming to the estate, and its cheerful yellow plastic, bright chrome, and rubber parts were glaringly out of place in the house. She placed the baby in it, adjusted the back so that Kierra could see from a comfortable semireclining position, then put a light blanket over her lap. Eleanor wondered if Lucas Matthews would be in the house, or if she might see Catherine, who had not come near her daughter for the past three days. *We must have the plague, little one*, she thought. Most of all, she wondered if perhaps she might see Michael Matthews, with whom she would eventually be having a meeting, in any case. The thought pleased her. *Maybe he does care. . . . I get the terrible feeling that I could just scoop up this child and take her away with me, and no one would know the difference except Mrs. Sanchez. And I doubt she would have an easy time making any one else care. What is wrong with them?* She looked down at the pretty baby. *Or with Kierra?* She pushed the stroller back to the hall.

"You don't expect me to tell you now, do you? Over the phone?" The words were muted, but they still carried to the hallway.

Eleanor stopped on her way down the hallway toward the kitchen where she thought she'd see if Mrs. Sanchez had located a food mill. She had forgotten the phone caller, whose voice grew more distant as she neared the library.

"I never said that, darling. Or, if I did, I was only joking, of course. I wouldn't say that to you, would I? No, I'd never say that to you. . . ." The voice caressed the words and transformed them into a teasing rebuff that was also a whispered promise. "You know what I *would* say to you. . . ."

The intimacy of the conversation made Eleanor uncomfortable. She wished she could make her passage known before she overheard anything more. But the deep carpet absorbed her footsteps and the sound of the stroller's wheels completely.

A low, throaty laugh seeped into the hallway. It and the distant ticking of a clock seemed to fill Eleanor's ears. The laugh, like the words, was highly personal, meant for the ears of a lover alone.

"I like it when you say that to me, darling," the

voice whispered. "Don't stop, tell me more. Yes, of course, now. I don't care. Don't be so paranoid. What more can they think of us, anyway?"

Cheeks burning, Eleanor improvised as best she could. "Now don't drop that blanket, Kierra," she said loudly.

The laughter broke off immediately.

"That's a good baby. Now let's see if we can find Mrs. Sanchez and get you some dinner." She reminded herself of a manic governess in a television skit, but she was desperate. "And then after dinner it'll be time for your nap!" she finished brightly just as she passed the doorway of the library.

Out of the corner of her eye Eleanor could see shining red hair and milk-white skin. Catherine Matthews was seated on the corner of a large wooden desk, the phone to her ear, her full red lips smiling into the receiver through a cloud of bluish smoke from the cigarette she held in her other hand.

"No, no, I'm still here. No, nothing. I can talk a little longer, darling."

The voice faded as they crossed the hallway and turned toward the living room.

"I guess your daddy isn't coming home right away after all," Eleanor said to the baby. She tried to shrug off a flash of disappointment. Her mind skipped from regret that Michael wasn't home, to the conversation she had overheard itself. More than making her uncomfortable, the playful dialogue between husband and wife had surprised the young nurse. Since she'd never seen Catherine and Michael Matthews together and had no real knowledge of their relationship, Eleanor knew that she had no basis for her surprise. But her imagination had already decided that the marriage had been a hastily made error of opposites who misread what they had seen in each other. It seemed likely that first pride and then the child had been holding them together. The scrap of conversation she had just overheard told her that *she* had been the one in error.

Suddenly struck by how little she really knew of Kierra's father, Eleanor realized that once again her flight of fancy had carried her far afield of the truth. *I'd never have imagined him involved in so . . . sensual and obviously uninhibited a phone conversation.* She thought of the quiet, serious man. *Never! A little mistake in personality analysis on my part.* But instead of laughing it off, she felt uncomfortable and mildly upset. *Why do I even care who or what Michael Matthews is, other than my new employer? Why do I feel slightly . . . betrayed, as if a friend has let me down?* she asked herself, moderately concerned.

She crossed the huge dining room, then doubled back through a smaller hallway, giving herself a moment more to think before going to the kitchen. She could faintly hear more of Catherine's seductive laughter stealing down the hallway.

Without meaning to, she began to think of her own past, as if to reach back and find some clue to her present confusion. *I'm thinking too much,* she told herself. *I'm creating an image of Dr. Matthews not how he is, but how I'd like him to be. It's because I'm lonely.* Again she sank back in time, finding the birth of her loneliness in a lifetime of waiting.

Since her teens she had been very busy, constantly working to pay for her education. She had little time for socializing and dates. Her loneliness had been shelved for the future.

All that had changed during her last year at school. She had gone to see her adviser concerning a clerical error about her credits, and she had fallen in love for the first time in her life. Ray White had been a sensitive and shy young man, with administrative genius and a sincere concern for the students with whom he worked. Even four years later she could think of Ray only at the cost of reliving some of her pain after his death. A young professor had offered him a ride home to northern California for the holidays in his private plane. He wanted her to come along and meet his family. But she had been committed to a part-time job and unhappily refused. Shortly after departure, the light craft was reported missing. What was left of the small plane was found several days later.

Somehow Eleanor had finished school. Mechanically, she found a job as a pediatrics nurse. She had no interest in men, but shared an apartment with two other nurses who were interested in little else. Rather than fight them, she went out on an occasional date. She knew that men found her attractive, but the loss of Ray created a scar that opened older wounds. She grew accustomed to loneliness and was content to pursue her career quietly. But even that grew sour when she discovered that she couldn't bear to see children hurt, suffer pain, die. At first she considered leaving nursing for good. But eventually she realized that the steady procession of children in and out of her life had become symbolic of the children she and Ray might have had. When one of her roommates told her of the opening in a father-and-son practice in general medicine, she went for an interview and gave her notice.

She was hired to work for Jim rather than his father, and although she found him attractive from the start, she knew he had a wife and family. She could not remember when she began to think of Jim as a friend rather than an employer, nor when their conversations had become heavy with unspoken messages. Once, after a ride home in a rainstorm, he had kissed her. From then on she had been on guard and it hadn't happened again. He didn't press, because he, like she, knew it was only a matter of time until the fence between them splintered under the weight of her own loneliness.

Instead, she had come to Bloodstone. And found herself fantasizing about another unattainable man. *I think they call that jumping from the pan into the fire,* she thought wearily, pausing in front of the kitchen door to tuck the light blanket back over the baby.

Whatever her past, Eleanor couldn't help but puzzle over the strong sense of frustration she felt. She couldn't accept Michael Matthews as the man who had been returning Catherine's sticky banter, yet she had no grounds for investing him with virtues he didn't possess. In fact she had little reason to feel anything but contempt for Kierra's father. Yet it still felt wrong. *Nothing fits in this house,* she told herself. *Everything's wrong here. Nothing makes sense. Not even me. Especially not me.*

The door to the kitchen opened just as she finished tucking in Kierra's blanket and smoothing the little arm over the crocheted duck. She looked up and gasped.

"Oh, I'm sorry, Eleanor. Did I startle you?"

Mutely rising from her knees, the girl shook her head. At the sight of him several things slid into perspective with an evil finality. Somehow she managed a smile of greeting for the rain-drenched Michael Matthews.

CHAPTER THREE

"**I**T'S REALLY COMING down out there!" He brushed rain from his dark hair. "Hello, Kierra."

Eleanor watched Michael bend over and touch the infant's cheek. His eyes held a curious mixture of softness and pain.

"Soon she'll be saying, 'Hi, Daddy!' She's doing really well."

The pained expression intensified as he stood up. "Good. I wanted to. . . ."

The kitchen door opened again and a small, pretty blonde woman in a trim suede pantsuit came into the room. A few drops of rain glistened on her carefully arranged hair. She studied Eleanor with feminine curiosity.

"Norma, this is Eleanor Lawrence, Kierra's nurse. Eleanor, this happens to be Forest Falls' first lady of real estate. And friend, Norma Vanowen."

Michael shrugged raindrops from the shoulders of his beautifully cut dark suit.

A saucy grin touched Norma's thin but well-shaped mouth. "That's the prettiest baby nurse I've ever seen. Hello, Eleanor, welcome to Forest Falls. What do you think of our mountains?"

Eleanor returned the smile and wondered what it was about the woman that immediately made her feel suspicious and vaguely defensive. "I love this house and what I've seen of the grounds, but I've hardly seen Forest Falls at all. What I have seen is beautiful, though." *She looks like an aging Sandra Dee, with shark's teeth!* Immediately she chided herself. *Soon I'll be meowing out loud.*

The real estate woman nodded with professional enthusiasm. "More than just being beautiful, this is also a most unique place to live and bring up a family. We have a two-room schoolhouse for our children. Perhaps you noticed it? A lovely stone cabin on the main road. Our community provides a clean, safe, smog-free environment that. . . ."

"Whoa, Norma," Michael interrupted, grinning down at her. "Eleanor isn't one of your potential customers. She's staying right here, remember?"

The blonde studied Eleanor silently for a moment, her smile bright and determined. "Why, yes, of course. To take care of Kierra." Then, as if remembering her manners, she kneeled by the child. "Hello, angel, how's Aunt Norma's little darling? My, aren't you a pretty little girl today."

Eleanor watched the woman waggle her fingers at her charge and a strong dislike put the final touch on her already negative feelings about Norma Vanowen. In spite of the woman's friendliness, artificiality dripped from her pores like saccharine from a dispenser. She also found herself slightly annoyed that an intelligent man like Michael Matthews couldn't recognize a phony like Norma when he saw one.

The blonde woman got up, brushed a speck of lint from her slacks, and beamed at the man by her side. "Michael, she's a darling. Look at those blonde curls!" She touched her own perfectly styled hair. "And hasn't she grown, though!" She put a slim pink-tipped hand on his arm.

"It's not so much that she's grown as how good she looks." He turned his serious dark eyes on Eleanor. "She looks like a different baby already, Eleanor. In so short a time. It's hard to believe. Do you have a moment to talk about her, or were you in a hurry?"

Norma touched his arm again. "Would you rather I come back later to talk to your grandfather? I do have a rather full schedule today. If this is going to take very long. . . ."

Michael shook his head. "Just a moment, unless Eleanor has something specific that needs talking about."

The young nurse shrugged. "Not really. Not at this point. Kierra's responding nicely to me. And she's begun to show some definite interest in objects and food. Her rash is greatly improved. I'm very pleased with her progress, Dr. Matthews. It . . . well, it's really more than I dared hope for in so short a time." She hesitated.

"Yes?"

"Well, it's just that. . . ."

A quick grin made his face appear several years younger. "Come on, Eleanor, you haven't pulled your punches on me before."

She had to smile back. Then she shrugged and her

face grew serious. She glanced quickly at Norma, who stood perfectly still like a mannikin, a vaguely bored look on her face. "Well, it's just that. . . . Well, no one's been in the nursery to see her in the time I've been here, and I think Kierra needs attention from her family. I know you've been away, but her mother and her great-grandfather haven't been in. Not once." She frowned. "She should be getting to know them; it would be very important for her emotional growth. At the same time I could be showing Mrs. Matthews the proper way to care for the child. She needs her family, Dr. Matthews."

A flash of sorrow crossed Michael's face. He kneeled by the baby again. "What's this?" He stood, the yellow duck in his hand.

Eleanor grinned. "That happens to be a duck. Doesn't he look a little like a duck? I made him for Kierra."

He turned the stuffed animal over in his large hands. "I think it looks very much like a duck, now that you mention it. I think it's an unusually handsome duck, in fact. Especially around the eyelashes. What do you think, Norma?"

Both turned to the blonde woman. Eleanor felt a faint surprise at the expression of jealousy on the realtor's face. At once the frown smoothed and broadened into a contagious smile. "I recognized it at once. You must teach me to do that someday, Eleanor." The smile deepened. She looked up at the man by her side. "Are we almost ready?"

"In a moment," Michael said absently, replacing the duck in its niche against Kierra's body. "I'll see what I can do about visitors." He studied Eleanor's face. "I can't make any promises. About anyone else, that is. I'll be in to see her every chance I can now that I'm home. There's urgent work I must do on my paper. The research is taking longer than I'd anticipated. But I'll try." His eyes dropped to the baby who returned his gaze with the frank interest of a curious infant.

Eleanor smiled warmly. "That will be a help. A great help. Come any time. Oh, we go for a walk around ten in the mornings and after two in the afternoons. We're in the nursery most of the time other than those few hours. I want her to be really familiar and feel totally safe in her environment." She didn't mention that she had already rearranged the furniture and decorated the room so that it would be like starting all over in a new environment for the child. "Kierra naps at eleven until one, and again at three or so. I put her down for the night between seven and seven-thirty. But feel free to come whenever you have the chance. She needs to know her father."

Norma threw a quick, incredulous look at the nurse, then glanced at Michael. Then her face assumed a visibly impatient appearance.

Michael returned Norma's glance, his face hard and unreadable. Then he nodded. "Fine. Thank you. We can talk more later. I'm . . . I'm really very pleased with Kierra. More than I can say." The solemnness dissolved with an unexpectedly boyish grin. "And with you."

She was undeniably pleased. After an exchange of insincere amenities by each woman, Eleanor and the baby continued on through the door to the kitchen in search of the food mill.

The dark-skinned young man turned and smiled broadly at the sight of the nurse and the stroller. He lifted a blackened rag from the bowels of the oven.

Eleanor inhaled the overpowering odor of oven cleaner and realized that she had been breathing in the scent of flowery cologne all the time she had been standing near Norma Vanowen. She herself preferred a subtle touch of vanilla extract, a trick she picked up from a Truman Capote book she had read in high school.

"Miss Lawrence! Are you looking for my mother? She is upstairs, I think."

"Actually," Eleanor said with a warm smile, "I was looking for a food mill. Your mother said there was one down here somewhere. Want to help me hunt? It might be quite a job." She looked around the cavernous kitchen at its dozens of drawers and cabinets. Abruptly she was feeling at the top of the world again, and the prospect of a good treasure hunt sounded like fun. It had been good to see the father of her charge again, even if he had been with that unpleasant woman. It was especially good to feel that someone other than herself cared about the well-being of the child. And she liked being with Ricardo. He seemed the most normal of everyone she had encountered at Bloodstone, the least weighed down with unspoken messages and cryptic comments. She gave him an especially bright smile. "Do you know what a food mill looks like?"

He puffed up his chest and tapped his head full of dark unruly curls. "Do I know! *Sí*, the kitchen is my domain! What I do not know could fill the head of a pin. All the rest, I know!"

She laughed. "Okay, then we hunt for the food mill."

He returned the laugh, exposing his unusually white and even teeth. "Nope. Mamacita is like an elephant. Give a request one time and she never

44

forgets." He reached under a butcher board counter and pulled out an old but serviceable food mill. "At your service, beautiful nurse." He bowed. "Sweet and lovely nurse."

She blushed slightly under the full face of his compliment. "I thank you, kind sir. Now I need a banana, an apple. . . ." She ticked off food possibilities on her fingers while the young Mexican scurried around the great kitchen locating things as she requested them. Deftly he put everything in a woven basket. "I'll bring them to the nursery at once."

"Oh, that's all right. I can carry that. It's not heavy."

The young man looked at her silently for a moment, an odd half smile on his face. When he spoke, his usually hardy voice was soft. "But you must have some of the compensations of the wealth here. I will carry your package."

"Compensations?" she asked, not understanding.

He shrugged. "People such as we think that the compensations of wealth are obvious." He looked around the kitchen. "This is sometimes only a half truth. There is no happiness here. Didn't you notice? There is only comfort." He wet his bottom lip, his eyes never leaving hers. "There are sad things here, secrets. Much fear. Learn to accept the comforts or you will find they have nothing else to give to you." His dark eyes dropped to the infant. "Many sad things. Many bad secrets." He looked back at her. "Believe me, they have nothing else to give you."

Eleanor rubbed her palms over the smooth wood of the butcher block, tracing the deep knife grooves in the middle with her fingertips. The spicy scent of hot red peppers made her wrinkle her nose and she glanced up at the wreath of them drying in the window. From far off came the high tinkling of a piano playing chamber music. "What secrets?"

Ricardo turned away from her and busied himself with the oven he had been cleaning when she arrived. "Life is full of secrets, *señorita*, is it not?"

"Yes . . . but. . . ."

He threw down the rag he was using. "I will take the basket to your room now."

She watched him leave the room. With a shrug, she wheeled the baby through the kitchen to the other door. On the way she poured herself a glass full of sparkling clear mountain water. She drank slowly and thought of what Ricardo had said. Her mind went to Catherine and Michael. Shrugging, she rinsed the glass and put it on the drainboard, then pushed Kierra back to the hall. She would go back upstairs and try a little fresh fruit for the baby's dinner. "You'll like it, sweetie. Much better than that old cereal."

The wheels made no sound on the carpet, and again she heard the seductive voice of Catherine Matthews wafting down the hall. Her laughter was musical, throaty, an insinuation of promised passion. "But darling, don't you think I remember?"

This time Eleanor made no attempt at announcing her passage. She pushed the stroller determinedly past the library, her head averted, her steps hurried. Catherine was Kierra's mother and Michael's wife, and Eleanor had no desire to hear the woman's conversation with her lover. In spite of her attempt at casualness, her face flamed as the voice dipped to a sexy whisper and she wondered if Michael, passing this way with Norma, had been subjected to this same outrage.

She tucked the stroller back in its niche and lifted the baby out of it. For a moment she hugged the infant, feeling the bonds tighten even more between herself and the tiny child in her arms. Ricardo had been right—this was a strange house. And into it she had come, determined to do what she could for a baby important to no one but herself. And perhaps now that she had opened his eyes, her own father. . . .

The fish tank glowed luminously, but on either side of the upper hallway was the opaque dimness that lengthened shadows and cast spells over Eleanor's imagination. She paused silently in front of the tanks to give Kierra a final view of the silvery creatures as they swam through their watery world. It was only when she turned that she realized she was not alone with the baby in the long hallway.

"Oh! I didn't realize anyone was there!" Embarrassment flooded her face with a crimson veil.

An edge of irritation penetrated Norma's otherwise calm voice as she stepped away from Michael in the dark hallway. "I was just leaving," she said smoothly.

Michael nodded.

Eleanor walked past them quickly, her head down, the baby tight in her arms. She opened the door to her room and gratefully slid inside. *What,* she wondered, *had they been doing in the hallway?* Had she seen them kiss, or was it only the impression she had garnered from Catherine's suggestive conversation on the telephone and Ricardo's cryptic comments in the kitchen? *Or,* she asked herself silently, *am I in the midst of a very modern marital scene in this very ancient estate?*

CHAPTER FOUR

THE MASSIVE BOULDERS behind the mansion seemed innocuous in the brilliant midday sun. Eleanor, remembering their strikingly sinister appearance on the night she had come to Bloodstone, eyed the rocky outgrowth with a speculative smile. A mythology buff all her life, she always tried to attach an allegorical significance to things which were not entirely clear to her. It was in her nature to find symbolic meanings when she could not find logical explanations. Much at Bloodstone was muddled and perplexing. Yet the estate itself was rapidly becoming more and more familiar and therefore less a threat, and the only menace she could see were the human forces which controlled the destiny of the great house in the forest. But the boulders seemed a separate entity, even under the beneficient light of day.

"Frightful, isn't it?" Catherine swirled her tall

glass and cocked an ear toward the tinkling ice cubes. "If I had my way I'd have them smashed into dust." She pushed her barely touched plate away from her and took a long pull on her drink. "Ugly monsters . . . am I next to smash my skull against them?"

"Drunk so early, my dear?" The rasping voice of Lucas Matthews carried no trace of warmth. He got up and crossed the patio to a serving table where he kept his cigarettes. "Damn fool game," he grumbled, walking stiffly back to his chair at the carved wooden table. He looked at the nearly empty pack through narrow eagle-sharp eyes that emerged from pockets of wrinkled, grayish flesh. "Damn doctor with his fool games."

Michael looked up from his plate. "He suggested you keep your cigarettes out of reach with the hope that you'd smoke less if they weren't so convenient." He shrugged. "It's for your own good, not his."

"And the damn fool died younger'n I am right now. And I'm still a long way from dead." His rough laughter boomed over the patio, then erupted in a short fit of convulsive coughing.

Eleanor watched the old man suck in a few lungsful of clear mountain air. "Well, your new doctor is still alive," she reminded him in a gentle voice, "and he wouldn't want you smoking, either." She checked his color from the other side of the table, then pushed Kierra's stroller farther out of the direct sun into the cooling shade of a great cedar tree. The curried shrimp was delicious, perfectly spiced and exquisitely set off by dried coconut, bits of chutney, large black raisins and hot salted peanuts. It was the first meal she spent with the family. *And friends,* she thought, glancing at

Norma Vanowen who picked delicately at her lunch as if wary of every fattening mouthful.

"This is just delicious!" Norma smiled brightly at the old man as he relit his cigarette. "Now Lucas, you've hardly touched your lunch at all!"

Catherine finished her drink, her eyes still on the huge boulders beyond the house. The tip of her pink tongue bathed her upper lip like a child going after the last drop of syrup. She got up and made herself another drink from the portable bar Ricardo had wheeled outside to them. "I'm not drunk," she said suddenly, turning to Lucas, her shoulder-length red hair flaming in the sun. "And if I was, what else is there to do here, anyway?" Her exquisite eyes were sullen.

A small brown and black chipmunk scampered between two tall fir trees and stood perfectly still, at once blending with the rich striping of the woods, the dry brown of the pine-needled earth and the angular grayness of jutting rocks and small, irregular stones, bits and pieces of the mountains which peered down on the patio from the south. Overhead, tapping with a staccato beat, a lone woodpecker punctured the silence.

"The rest of us find things to do," the old man answered dryly, a cold light in his fading eyes. He tapped some ash from his cigarette into a planter by his chair. "Just as you've . . . found something to do."

"Grandfather," Michael said tightly. He glanced at Norma who was concentrating hard on her plate, then met Eleanor's frankly inquisitive stare. He turned back to Lucas. Both men exchanged glances but neither spoke.

Eleanor tried to read the unspoken words that flashed between the elder Matthews and his grandson. She knew that Catherine was at the base of their dissension, but she sensed that there was more, much more, below the surface. She could feel an enmity between men who had so obviously shared only love until recently. Now the wall between them stood high and thorny, and to the young nurse it seemed that Catherine, cool and aloof, cared for neither. Unconsciously Eleanor shivered. Her hand reached out and stroked the baby asleep in the stroller. The chipmunk took flight toward the patio, then—as if aware of the tensions—ran back toward the wilderness, scurrying off to a sloping field of orange wild flowers that clustered colorfully at the base of a giant cedar. From somewhere nearby came the muted rumbling of rocks striking the ground and each other. "What's that?" she asked, her hand tightening on the baby's shoulder.

"Oh, just a small avalanche," Norma said, determinedly pushing her plate away. "If you listen you'll be hearing them all the time up here. The mountains are safe enough, but rather unstable."

Eleanor nodded as if answered not to her spoken words but to a question she had been asking since her arrival at Bloodstone the very first time. *Unstable. There's something here that's terribly unstable, as if everyone and everything is heaped up in an unstable order on the edge of some terrible explosion.* She sipped at her coffee cup, absorbed in a sudden fear that struck her with psychic intensity. *Someone is going to die here! Something terrible will happen . . . has happened before . . .will have to happen again. . . .* The coffee burned her lip; her eyes stung.

She chose her words with uncharacteristic care, looking instinctively at Michael Matthews. "This is a beautiful but strange area. In spite of its loveliness, it would make an ideal setting for a good old-fashioned horror story or some terrible murder mystery. I can't help but think this house has a special and perhaps terrible history." She waited, but only the woodpecker responded. She listened to the tapping silently for a moment, then started again. "Am I wrong?"

Norma turned an especially bright smile toward Eleanor. "You have quite an imagination, haven't you? I don't think this is an especially morbid or dramatic area and this estate is just beautiful. Of course, really large homes like Bloodstone. . . ."

"How did it come to be called Bloodstone?" Suddenly she grinned at her own pushiness. The self-consciousness she would ordinarily feel was obliterated by the lure of her fired imagination. Overhead, giant trees cast spells over the patio, and Eleanor again looked at the huge cluster of rock just beyond.

"Actually, you're right about this house," the gruff voice of Lucas Matthews held a trace of amusement. "I like a woman who asks when she wants to know something." His thin lips curled with a tight smile. "The original owner, man by the name of St. Clair, died by hitting his head on those rocks back there. The locals took to calling the estate Bloodstone, because they claim the stone takes on the color of blood during the full moon." His laugh again ended in a racking cough.

Norma nodded.

Catherine's high-pitched laughter chased away the last of Lucas' amusement. "Oh, this place is a real winner. Tell her about the next owners and how the husband shot himself against those rocks."

"An accident," Lucas muttered, not looking at his grandson's wife. "A damn fool accident."

"Or why don't you tell her about the young man who bought this treasure and came home to find his pregnant wife frozen to death on those same rocks? Or about the boy from town who got drunk and fell from them. Don't you want to tell stories to the pretty nursemaid you bought to care for your great-granddaughter?" Catherine's laughter swelled, rippling the forest air with its cold hysteria.

Michael got up suddenly, his chair falling backward behind him.

But Catherine stood first. "Never mind seeing me inside, darling," she said icily. "I'm on my way for a brief nap." She finished her drink and turned the same frosted eyes to Eleanor. "I trust I've answered your questions, my dear. We're a rather . . . reclusive family, and we aren't always as cordial as we might be." Her laugh was contemptuous and her gaze fell to her husband.

Kierra turned in her sleep and her eyes slowly opened. It was past time for her bottle. So Eleanor quickly lifted her from the stroller and cuddled her on her lap, one hand going to the diaper bag for the waiting formula. "I . . . I think it's at least a colorful history." She averted her eyes from the rock.

Eleanor watched Catherine walk back towards the house without a glance in the direction of her child. She had looked forward to this lunch as an opportunity to talk to the beautiful red-haired woman about Kierra, and hopefully, establish some sort of commitment on the mother's part about regular daily visits to the nursery so that Kierra could come to know and trust her mother. And the woman would learn, under Eleanor's tactful tutelage, how to properly care for her infant. *But she doesn't care at all,* the young nurse realized, frustration and pity competing with irrepressible anger at so cold a mother.

She looked around at the others, her frustration growing. In spite of his domineering mannerisms she was coming to rather like the taciturn old man, yet there was no warmth in him for his great-grandchild. She looked at the overly sweet real estate agent who was once again picking at her plate between glances at Michael. She, alone, had given Kierra some concentrated attention at the onset of the luncheon, but Eleanor had been skeptical of the sugary words and tickling fingers. *Where had Norma been when the baby was slowly starving?* Only in Michael Matthews did she detect the slightest indication of genuine feeling for the infant. *Even there, something's wrong!* She couldn't identify what she felt, but she sensed a strange reluctance that somehow got in the way of a normal closeness between father and daughter. *Something's wrong everywhere I look!* Again the incongruity of Michael and Catherine as a couple set off her curiosity. She had a hundred questions revolving around Catherine's phone conversation and the presence of Norma Vanowen in this house, so solidly at Michael's side. *Who are these people really? What's going on here?*

While urging the bottle on a grudgingly hungry Kierra, Eleanor covertly studied Michael from under her long pale lashes. He interested her. She couldn't deny it. There was something about him that drew her, that intrigued her. His somber good looks and Alan Alda masculinity were not the major attraction, although Eleanor was very aware of them. If he had been a young man that she met in the office or at a party, his appearance would have been enough to stir her interest. But here at the picturesque and oddly disturbing estate, as the obviously disturbed husband of a fiery, alcoholic, and contemptuous woman—as the father of an infant that should not have been in the condition Eleanor had found her—the nurse looked deeper than surface appearances—wondering not for the first time why, in the midst of so much negative evidence, she felt so strong an attraction toward the man.

Impulsively, she hugged Kierra to her, protecting her from evil forces that seemed to disguise themselves in the beings from whom the child should ordinarily expect the most comfort and care. She distrusted and disliked Catherine, felt certain that Norma, the ever-smiling realtor, wanted something and was playing a game with all of them. She felt comfortable about the servants in the great house, although Ricardo's cryptic words the day before had disturbed her greatly. Lucas Matthews used power as some men used their hands—to accomplish the simplest of acts. *And Michael,* she thought, *who is this man? Kind or cunning? What secrets does he hold? Why do I care?*

"She *is* looking better. I could swear she's gained weight since I left."

Eleanor roused herself from her thoughts and looked up into Michael's dark eyes as he settled into the seat vacated by his wife next to the nurse. She saw that Lucas and Norma were deep in conversation, Norma's slim hand dipping into a brown briefcase and emerging with a sheaf of neatly typed papers. She removed the bottle from Kierra's relaxed mouth and brought the baby to her shoulder.

"She has." A bubble of air came immediately, and Eleanor popped the bottle back into the tiny mouth. "She really is doing so much better, Dr. Matthews. It's not very professional of me, I know, but, oh, I just feel so sure that it will be no time at all until Kierra's completely well and responding like any other baby her age!"

She couldn't keep the excitement from her voice as she beamed down at the beautiful infant. "This morning she kept raising her hands toward the mobile I put up over her crib, and while she's still not crying for food or accepting the bottle with any real eagerness, she ate most of a banana before and drinks twice as much formula as she did when I came. I was sure she'd respond to me, but I had no expectations that it would be this soon!"

His eyes on her were soft, yet the same pain was there. "You should have children of your own."

She looked away from him, remembering Ray, instantly thinking of the children they might have had. Her mind passed over the sick and dying children she had cared for professionally, then she thought of the children that belonged to Jim Munroe and the woman to whom he was committed. She touched the soft curls of the infant in her arms and felt a longing unlike any she had ever known before. "I feel a little as if Kierra were really mine, Dr. Matthews. I know that sounds strange, but I feel very close to Kierra already. I *know* I can help her! That's a little like giving her life, isn't it?" Suddenly her face flamed as the intimacy of her words came back at her`. . . the secrets she had given up to a man she hardly knew, a man she had no tangible reason to trust.

He looked at her carefully, then reached out and

touched the child in her arms. His voice, when he spoke, was tinged with bitterness. "It's more, Eleanor, it's far more. Any animal in the field can give birth to something. And it can leave its young to die in the field, also. What does it take to be a mother?" The bitterness changed to an emotion that bordered on agony. "Or a father?" he asked with a quiet intensity. "Or a father. . . ." His eyes, on the child, were filled with sadness and terrible conflict. "Poor sweet little thing . . . what did she do to deserve us?"

Eleanor was suddenly suffused with a sense of great personal tragedy. Only her stubborn interest in the man kept her from acute embarrassment at unexpectedly witnessing such private torment. She felt as if the two of them had been abruptly swept off on a sea of emotion and revelation, and while neither knew the specific source of the other's pain, each somehow shared a common bond of vulnerability. It was all she could do to keep from reaching out to him, taking his hand, offering the comfort of her arms. She had felt such emotions but had never been called upon to share them; something about the desperation and loneliness in Michael Matthews voice called up her own soul, as if to merge with another.

With a great effort, Eleanor drew away from the pull of Michael's bright eyes. She averted her head and noticed Mrs. Sanchez at work in the small vegetable garden alongside the house where she grew her own herbs. The earthy woman's slightly thickening body, bent over the soil, was like a touch of welcome reality. She watched the housekeeper weed the garden and felt a calmness descend over her. *Jim's right. I have a fertile imagination and here, in this atmospheric house, I'm allowing it to carry me to crazy, illogical places.* A radiant butterfly with iridescent wings of blue and green settled on a plant near the stooping woman, and Eleanor thirstily drank in the prettiness of the scene while Kierra nuzzled at the bottle. She felt a warmth and comfort in the presence of the motherly housekeeper, Then, without warning, the bubble burst as Mrs. Sanchez, calmly and without expression, suddenly reached up and brought a rock down on the butterfly, crushing it with a carefully aimed blow.

"What's wrong? What's the matter?"

Eleanor looked up at the man by her side who, looking at her, had not noticed the housekeeper at all. "I . . . I. . . ." She felt a wave of sickness, as much at the sudden shattering of the image of normalcy she had built as at the unneccessary, senseless cruelty she had so unexpectedly witnessed. "Nothing. It's . . . nothing." She tried a smile.

As they locked gazes, Eleanor noticed the deep silence. Where the steady drone of Lucas' comments had counterpointed with Norma's higher-pitched voice, now there was only the distant sounds of the forest itself. She turned to find both the old man and Norma staring oddly at herself and Michael. The elder Matthews' weathered face reflected fathoms of unreadable speculation, but Norma Vanowen's face revealed only a cold jealousy.

From the doorway, a fresh drink in her hand, Catherine Matthews broke the heavy silence with her laughter.

CHAPTER FIVE

LONG SHADOWS SLICED across patches of yellow sunlight, chopping the day into splinters of sudden evening and blinding dawn. Blinking rapidly and feeling rather like Alice after tasting the drink-me potion, Eleanor pushed the stroller and made her way along a well-worn path, while admiring the mammoth trees and beyond, the pressing, awesome mountains.

The earth was pungently alive, rich with new life and energy after the summer storm. The young nurse inhaled the heady scent and felt a great contentment take precedence over the concerns which had been cluttering her mind. This was what she liked best, being alone with Kierra in the majestic wilderness, utterly safe in the forest's womb, satisfied to accept the physical reality of being alive without the confusing complications of intellect. It was enough to bask in the pleasures of the moment, and for once allow the sun and the magical beauty of nature to blot out everything that carried confusion or pain. Her mind reacted by stretching lazily, its tentacles wriggling like a flower breaking free of the ground. It shrugged off its cares one by one, bathing itself in the simplicity of the moment.

"Look at that, Kierra!" She stopped and turned the stroller so that the baby could see the large outcropping of jagged rock which, incredulously, sported an amazing growth of frail and exquisite yellow blossoms with dainty green stems and short, waxy leaves. "Isn't it pretty!" She bent to grin at the child, then saw that Kierra was sound asleep. "Well, so much for the schedule."

She watched a moment longer, then began to walk on. Now that the baby was asleep, there was no reason to go back to the nursery. *The air will do her good, and it won't hurt me, either,* she decided, stepping over a cluster of pale lavender flowers.

She hadn't slept well the night before. Since her lunch on the patio with the family she had felt restless and out of sorts, unsure of her own powers of perception. The image of that motherly brown hand, so competent and gentle. . . . She shuddered, yet the picture of the rock crushing the innocent butterfly would not dissolve. It had infiltrated her dreams and shattered her self-confidence. She found herself doubting everyone in the house of being what they seemed, and it especially took all of her will to communicate with Mrs. Sanchez. It was a joyous relief to escape the house and its members, to wheel her precious charge away from the atmosphere of darkness and deception.

The walking path broke off in three different directions. An overhanging of vines and blackberry bushes narrowed one lane impassably. A second way led to the rear of the estate, opening onto the huge boulders which had given Bloodstone its name. Remembering the stories Catherine had told the day before, Eleanor was quick to turn the stroller to the third path, one which led to and then paralleled the main road leading to the actual town of Forest Falls. She glanced back and saw the massive house looming over the mountain terrain. It was like a black shadow on her consciousness, somehow occult and threatening, as if the lives that had been sacrificed on the altar of its sentinel rocks lived on in some ghostly vaporous existence, darkening and cooling the house and its present family, intangibly demanding retribution. She moved quickly from the omnipotent structure, seeking safety in the fragrant forest, in the rays of the warming sun. A large yellow and orange butterfly dipped down from the trees and hovered over a patch of periwinkles. Pushing yesterday's experience resolutely from her thoughts, she watched the beautiful insect play. The butterfly's wings trembled over a blue flower and Eleanor wished the baby was awake to enjoy this sudden splash of color. Then, like a wary soldier holding his territory, a pale brown spider climbed a flat leaf near the butterfly. It appeared to study the hovering insect, seemingly mesmerized by its color and wing span.

"*Lycosa carolinensis* . . . fierce hunters of the spider world, but that fellow's a bit too big for him."

Eleanor gasped and turned.

"Sorry. I didn't mean to startle you. I saw you looking at the butterfly and the spider." Michael Matthews looked down at the sleeping baby.

The nurse smiled. "*Lycosa . . . cara . . . cara. . . .*"

The tall man rolled up the cuff of his blue work shirt and reached out, capturing the spider and the leaf in his palm. *"Lycosa carolinensis* . . . wolf spider, as it's better known. They're the hunters. They actually pursue their prey instead of waiting for food to ensnare themselves in their nets. See, this one probably lives on the underside of this damp leaf, or maybe under one of those nearby rocks." He watched the butterfly flit away, then carefully replaced the spider and a bit of ripped leaf on the broad avenue of a larger leaf of the same plant. "Some *Lycosa carolinensis* build tunnels and some do spin webs, but these are the exceptions. Most, like our friend here, are hunters."

Eleanor absently rocked the stroller and stared mistily at the spider which seemed frozen in place, perhaps pausing to take stock of itself. "The myth goes that there was once a very beautiful queen in a great kingdom who prided herself on the beauty of the garments she could weave from fine silks. She was certain that no other woman could weave as flawless and marvelous a cloth. Then one day she got word of a simple peasant girl who was not only extraordinarily pretty, but who had a wide reputation for weaving exceptionally lovely cloth. At once the queen ordered the girl to be brought to her and then declared that they would have a contest." She smiled at him. "They locked themselves in a room and when they were done the judging began. It turned out that there was no one who could say that the weaving done by the peasant girl was any less exquisite then the work done by the queen, and of course no one dared say more. But the queen was also a very powerful witch. Immediately she turned the girl into an insect. But out of respect for the peasant girl's talents, she turned her into a spider, so that she might spend eternity weaving her beautiful patterns."

She looked up to find Michael studying her closely, the same soft, wondering smile on his face. Immediately she felt a twinge of embarrassment and again damned her playful imagination.

"You're a very beautiful girl, Eleanor, do you know that?"

She smiled uncomfortably and looked away from the flattering warmth in his eyes. Her mind, suspicious after yesterday's treachery in the garden, brought up images of Catherine and Norma, then the likeness of Kierra when Eleanor had seen her for the very first time. She found it easier to harden herself to the attraction she felt for him. "Thank you, Dr. Matthews," she said with a certain stiffness. "But I'm not beautiful. Mrs. Matthews is beautiful." She couldn't bring herself to include Norma Vanowen in the category of beautiful women, though she had to admit to herself that the blonde was exceptionally attractive. The realtor struck the girl as a well-done fakery, and the smile Norma wore seemed made of porcelain and paint. Whatever confusion she felt about Catherine as a person, at least her feelings for Norma Vanowen were clearly definable—she disliked and distrusted her.

He appeared not to notice the stiffness. He looked at her openly, the faint smile fading. "I liked your story. It makes me realize how much I've learned and how little I know. And please call me Michael, not Dr. Matthews. My grandfather could buy his way into society if he chose, but he was not born to it, nor will he or the rest of us ever be comfortable there among the stuffy set."

She looked up at him through her dark lashes. He seemed different out there among the trees in his casual shirt and dark corduroy trousers. He seemed younger, less composed. *For the first time he seems almost happy,* she thought. *Almost at peace with himself.*

"And you *are* beautiful, you know. No, not in the way my wife is beautiful. Hers is a cold, brittle beauty, a beauty that seems to be an end in itself . . . self-appeasing, sterile, ungiving. Hers is a beauty to look at, to admire, perhaps even to want to own, like a painting that will disintegrate in time. But yours is a beauty that will grow and mature, will deepen with time and age. Yours is a beauty to touch. . . ." He broke off, his fine lips closing suddenly as if to. bite back his words.

Eleanor saw the loneliness that was in the man and it touched off her own. Her heart raced desperately and the air, stealing into her lungs through her suddenly constricted throat, tasted sweet and hot. At once she felt afraid. She looked down at the sleeping child and blinked back an irrepressible tear. "I . . . I was just taking the baby for a walk. This path follows the main road, doesn't it?" She turned and began pushing the stroller again, not looking back to see if he were following or still standing near the bush. The spider was gone.

"Yes," he said, falling into step next to her, his face averted.

She wanted to erase his obvious embarrassment and groped helplessly for a word which would tell him that she hadn't been offended. *Yet it's equally important to keep a certain, professional formality in our relationship,* she told herself, wheeling

Kierra around the splintered trunk of a fallen tree.

"I . . . I'm sorry, Eleanor. I shouldn't have talked that way." The tall man slowed his pace to match hers. "When I'm home and can find the time, I go for long walks around the estate. It's the only time I can really think, and I'm afraid I was doing some fairly deep, personal thinking just before I met you. I . . . I don't want you to think that I'm some kind of. . . ."

She blushed and quickly interrupted him. "I'm flattered that you could be married to such a beautiful woman and think that I'm also beautiful. I like compliments like any other woman. Even if I am a nurse." She laughed and felt the tension drain from her body, yet at the same time she couldn't help thinking of Norma. Again she wondered at the relationship between the realtor and her employer. "And I don't think you meant anything by what you said."

He walked silently for a moment. "I did mean what I said, though. About beauty, about my wife. It's very difficult for me to think about my wife and beauty at the same time."

Eleanor digested his statement. Again she let curiosity supersede her own natural shyness. "Things . . . and people . . . either grow more or less beautiful with time and association. I think that physical beauty is like icing on a cake. No matter how good it is, there has to be something underneath or it loses its appeal in a hurry."

He didn't smile. "People buy cakes because they look good. They even fool themselves into believing there's something underneath when there isn't, if they like the icing enough." He stopped and touched her arm. "Beauty should be restricted to art, to . . . things. It shouldn't have anything to do with human relationships. Companionship ... the sharing of ideas and ideals ... that's what a relationship should be about."

Because he had stated so exactly what she herself desired in a relationship beyond all else, she was silent. Turning, she began to walk again, casually breaking the contact between his hand and her arm. She knew that Michael was expanding a lesson he had learned since and as a result of his marriage, and she wanted a quiet moment to think about the man, about who he was, and how he had come to be who he was. Her mind felt clouded and syrupy, her flesh throbbing with awareness where his hand had touched her. Forcing herself to think, she tried to imagine Michael as a boy, growing up on this estate, estranged from the community by wealth. *And,* she suspected, *the iron hand of his grandfather.* She wondered at his parents and his past, intuitively knowing that he had been very much alone in his life and was—still—alone. Whatever his relationship to Norma Vanowen, Eleanor suspected that the pretty blonde was no greater cure for his loneliness than his wife had proven to be. Again she felt a correlating loneliness in herself. She thought of Jim and knew that he had only increased that private loneliness. . . . Then she knew it was time to change the subject. Past time. A heady lightness was in her step and she felt suddenly afraid that if the intimacy between them continued, she would lose herself in emotions that she had no right to feel.

"Mrs. Sanchez said you were in Los Angeles, working. I don't know what a historian does. Do you teach?" she asked, deliberately changing the subject.

He stared at her a moment, his eyes aware of the

maneuver but willing to go along with it. "Some historians teach. Some work for museums, libraries, and universities. Others do research. When I got my PhD, I was given a research grant from the university to do a definitive study of this area of the San Bernardino mountains. There's a great deal of fascinating history connected with the gold rush in Holcomb Valley, and at one time this entire area was controlled by Chinese who had great hopes of establishing a great health resort. Forest Falls itself used to be the hangout for the movie stars who liked taking their pleasure in gambling and women." He smiled. "A few of the old houses up here were places of business, and I understand that business was good."

"From what Mrs. Matthews was saying, it sounds like Bloodstone has quite a history of its own." She stooped to pick up a rock that was streaked with green.

"That's jade. There's quite a bit of it around here. It's very low-grade, though. There are also garnets and geodes. Have you ever seen a geode? They look like coconuts made of rocks, and when they're sliced open. . . ."

"Oh! They're all purple inside, like a cave made of purple crystals! When I was a little girl my father once bought me one for my birthday. I kept it on a stand in my bedroom." She fell silent, remembering the geode and what happened to it. "Then one day my brother, in a fit of rage over some confrontation with our stepfather, threw the geode to the ground, smashing it." She shrugged and went back to thinking about Bloodstone. "Does the estate really have a history of strange deaths?"

He nodded and waited until they had skirted a

large rock before going on. "Robert St. Clair was believed to have been murdered. The locals think it was Bloodstone itself that got him, and the police rather thought it was his business partner who did it at the time. I don't really know how the investigation turned out. He was found at the foot of those ugly boulders with his head smashed in, a pool of blood over the rock. He was already dead. The boulders do have a reddish cast in the moonlight, probably because of the high clay content of the earth up here. At any rate, it was discovered that prior to his death, St. Clair had mysteriously sold off a good slice of the estate to his groundskeeper's young son for cash, and the money was never accounted for, which could indicate robbery as a motive.

"The second death was an apparent accident, though I understand there was some suggestion that the man was a suicide. I suppose he thought the rocks made as good a death site as any. He certainly couldn't have found anything to hunt so close to the house."

"And the pregnant woman?" She was fascinated by the morbid tale, again struck by the extreme power the house seemed to hold over the land. Beyond the beauty and value of the structure, she could feel something akin to personality, a pervading iciness, a domineering force, as if the mansion were waiting and watching.

Michael ran his palm over the dry trunk of an ailing pine tree whose branches, far above, were sparsely dressed in green. The heavy scent so reminiscent of vanilla extract hung in the air around the huge tree. "The smog is slowly killing these old trees. Each year it drifts higher and higher, and the trees fight less and less." He sighed deeply. "That was really terrible. There was a great storm one winter and the road was washed away. The elevation climbs rapidly at this end of the canyon, so that when the beginning of the canyon is just getting inches of snow we might be buried under a foot or more up here. That's why we keep a jeep as well as the Mercedes and the station wagon.

"Anyway, the road had washed away and the young husband, afraid that his wife would go into labor, set out on foot to get help. The phone lines were down and shortly after he left the power lines went as well. That happens during winter storms even now, which is why we put in our own generator. Anyway, with the power went the heat. Though it's propane, of course, the heating system at the time was generated by an electrical starter. The wife tried to keep warm by burning wood, but she couldn't lift the logs for the fireplaces and she couldn't split them for the stoves, either. She was alone in the dark and the cold, and she had already been ill. Apparently she started labor sometime during that night."

Eleanor immersed herself in the story, imagining the fear the pregnant woman must have felt as she waited for her husband and help to arrive.

"About a mile from the house the husband slipped and twisted his ankle, slowing his progress on the icy road. The houses nearby were all vacated by people fearing that the storm would imprison them, and though he tried every door, there was no one to help him. Half frozen and in terrible pain, he broke into one of the houses, discovered that their phone was also out of service, and sat down to rest and get warm before setting out again. He fell asleep in the chair from exhaustion, and it was morning before he awakened."

Eleanor conjured up a vision of the wife, her labor pains growing steadily closer, waiting through the black night, feeling the freezing cold that penetrated whatever covers she could put on. She imagined the house itself, a giant animal perching threateningly over the terrified young woman, its silence total and eerie during the endless night. *At what point,* she wondered, *did the laboring woman run from the monster?* She shuddered.

"For some reason—who knows? She was in labor and probably half crazed with fear and pain. For whatever reason, at some point during the night or in the early morning, the woman left the house and wandered around the estate, falling from time to time, getting up and going on, then falling again. Her tracks were everywhere, running in circles, like a caged animal. She must have come to the rocks a hundred times, they say, and finally she could move no more. She sat in the snow at the foot of the boulders while the snow continued to fall, her labor probably unnoticed by then. Perhaps she slept.

"By the time her husband, himself suffering from frostbite and a bad sprain, found help and returned, it was well into the next night. They found her dead by the rocks." He shook his head and helped Eleanor to carefully maneuver the stroller over a sprinkling of rocks so that the infant wouldn't be roused from her slumber.

"How terrible! No wonder the house is called Bloodstone." She sighed. "And a local boy also died here? On the rocks again?"

He nodded. In the distance a bird took flight in the tree tops, rustling the leaves and disturbing the quiet. "He was drunk and by that time the house was uninhabited. Kids came by whenever they got brave enough, breaking a few windows and climbing the rocks. No serious damage was ever done, though, because everyone stayed a little afraid of Bloodstone, drunk or sober. This poor kid was only sixteen. He lived a week after his fall." He stopped and turned back toward the house. High above the trees was the long tip extending from the cupola and the very tops of the twin turrets. "You know, I've lived in that house since my mother died when I was nine years old. It's the only home I've ever known. Yet there's something about it, something strange and strong. When I was a boy I would awaken with nightmares. In each of them the house, like an armed warrior, would be advancing on me, tightening around me. . . ." He turned and smiled at the nurse. "Kids have active imaginations."

She frowned. "I felt something about the house the other morning, when it was raining. I felt . . . like the house knew all about me, and somehow didn't approve very much."

His laugh was warm. "Now that has to be imagination. Even Grandfather approves of you, and I can't say that about very many people. Not even Norma, who's trying to help him."

Eleanor wrinkled her brow. "Is he trying to sell Bloodstone?"

The young historian shook his head and his handsome, cleanly executed features took on an expression of mock horror. "Sell! My grandfather sell Bloodstone! Never!" His gaze drifted to another of the ailing pines and his face smoothed. "My grandfather is a headstrong man who insists on getting what he wants. He is determined, for reasons I'm not sure I understand, to restore Bloodstone to its former size. When the first owner sold off part of the land he chopped the estate to about two-thirds its original property. Since then the land has been subdivided and resold, with six homes and a large entertainment complex containing rental cabins, a small grocery store and a large saloon which features live music down the road. It's not my kind of place, but the owner has every right to run his business on his own land."

Eleanor glanced quickly at Michael. In spite of the calm logic of his words, something in his voice had betrayed great tension and something else she was at a loss to define.

"That leads back to the house, if you'd like to return." He pointed to a dusty path veering off to the left.

She hesitated. It was so nice to be in the woods with Michael. In spite of the emotions he raised in her, there was something relaxing in being with him that she had never experienced with Jim. She glanced at the baby and knew that soon she would be waking, and she was training the little girl to expect food as soon as she stirred. Knowing the extreme importance of routine at this point in the infant's development, Eleanor nodded and turned the stroller gently toward the other path.

Kicking a sharp stone out of the way of the wheels, Michael resumed talking. "My grandfather has been determined to get back the land for as long as I can remember. I think the first mistake he made was misjudging the prudent types of people with whom he was dealing. He immediately bought up one of the homes, and right away he had the house completely destroyed, since his intention was to restore the estate to what it had been before it was subdivided. If he had waited and bought up all the land first, he might have gotten away with it. But when the others saw that first house destroyed for no reason other than to give Lucas Matthews a larger estate, their sense of indignation and waste was aroused. Oh, Grandfather got the other houses. But he paid through the nose for each one. They laughed at him and held what he wanted high over his head, and he bit, hating them for making him beg. But it was that important to him.

"The largest parcel of land and the one closest to the house itself was still owned by Jason Reed, the groundskeeper's son. He had a shack on the land at the time, and he was adamant in his refusal to sell the land to my grandfather. It turned into a grudge war, with each man moving past logic in their desire to best the other. I always had the strangest feeling that the two of them knew each other long before the land deal, and that the land was a symbol for something else they had between them." He shrugged. "Maybe not. My grandfather denies it. He hates Jason for standing in the way of his restoring Bloodstone to its original status."

"Does Jason Reed own the saloon and cabins?" She dimly recalled passing the place on her way to Bloodstone. A cloyingly sweet smell assaulted her nostrils and she hurried past a great bank of wild lilacs, appreciating the blurred lavender blossoms but overwhelmed by the strong smell. She slowed once she was out of the direct line of their powerful fragrance. The baby stirred and made a small sound.

"Not anymore. While my grandfather was in England on some business, Jason became ill and sold the land to someone from down the hill, Ken Fletcher." His lips seemed to curl over the name. After a moment the dark shadow left his face. He continued in a calm voice. "It was done very quietly, and when my grandfather returned, he found the saloon already completed and the cabins under construction on what he insists on calling his land." He paused and held back a branch that had grown across the path. Its green fingers and whiplike arm cast a long shadow over the path, obscuring their view until they reached a break in the trees and the sun slashed through the straining branches in long yellow streaks.

"Your grandfather must have been terribly upset." The strong light permeated Kierra's lids, and she blinked her eyes rapidly, her blonde little head twisting away from the brightness. Eleanor hurried her toward the shadows.

"My grandfather's been terribly upset from the day he was born. He was livid when Jason wouldn't sell the land, but when he found that a saloon was established on the land he was almost out of his mind with rage. I'm only surprised that he didn't kill Jason Reed and Ken Fletcher at the time." His laugh was sardonic. "That's only because Jason was in the hospital dying of cancer anyway, and Fletcher kept well out of sight at the time." Again the bitterness twisted his features. "But he didn't keep out of sight for long." He added the last softly, under his breath.

"And Norma?" Eleanor wondered what was between the saloon owner and the historian. But she sensed that Michael would tell her what he wanted her to know without her asking.

"Norma hates having a saloon up here almost as

74

much as my grandfather does, and she's very fond of him, too. She has come up with a plan to help my grandfather get what he wants." He looked at Eleanor, hesitated, then continued. "It's very confidential and very important to the old man. Restoring Bloodstone is his one dream, the final act he wants to complete before he dies." He looked at her searchingly.

"I understand."

Satisfied, he went on. "Norma has found herself some contractor who's willing to buy the saloon land as well as Bloodstone in name only, supposedly to turn it into a development of exclusive homes, something like a mountain Bel-Air. The highway is being rebuilt which means that Forest Falls will be far more accessible to the city. The idea is that Fletcher is supposed to sell his land at a good price through Norma. The deal will seemingly fall through and my grandfather will buy the land back from Norma's contractor.

"However, it's not going that simply. Fletcher wants Bloodstone to go on the block first. He wants to see my grandfather's name on the bill of sale before he'll consider signing away his land. And that means going through escrow. Of course my grandfather wants to negotiate the deal strictly on paper, without actually releasing the estate."

Eleanor saw that the baby was once again soundly sleeping now that she was out of the sun. "But if the offer is a good one, why won't Fletcher sell? For that matter, why won't he just sell directly to your grandfather?"

The cloud returned to Michael's dark eyes. "There are . . . personal reasons why Bloodstone won't do business with the saloon directly, and why Fletcher would never sell to us."

There was so much she wanted to know about the family—about him. Just the presence of Michael by her side was exciting. She was beginning to feel as if she had known him forever, and yet logic told her she knew him not at all. The facts about this man by her side were at dramatic odds to her intrusive feelings about the man. She had to remind herself of the pathetic condition of Kierra before she had taken over. *What is it I feel for him,* she asked herself, *that repudiates my logic and makes me see this man in a different light from the others here?* The answer was painfully clear. *I like him! In spite of my feelings about Kierra's condition, I like him. So immediately I set about redesigning him and recasting his personality to suit myself! And that image doesn't include loving a drunken wife who would mistreat her own baby. Yet he did marry her and he's still with her. It's wrong of me to make excuses for him to myself . . . to absolve him for Kierra.* But Kierra was only part of it. Michael Matthews had been very much on her mind since she had come to the hauntingly beautiful estate. He was becoming increasingly important to her. His handsome features and aristocratic bearing was etched in her thoughts more indelibly than she'd realized. Suddenly she felt depressed. To have escaped an entanglement with Jim to find herself allowing an attraction for another married man was more than she could endure. *And where was I placing myself in this little fantasy?* she asked herself harshly. *I've taken on the role of protective mother with Kierra, tossing aside my professional objectivity. Have I subconsciously been planning on dumping the present Mrs. Matthews in some ditch and slipping into her shoes when I get the chance?*

The path joined with another and broadened, and they walked a short distance in silence, then came to the base of the massive boulders where four people had met their untimely deaths. Eleanor shuddered. Then she looked up to see the tall muscular figure of Jim Munroe waiting for her at the end of the path.

CHAPTER SIX

THE LOCAL DINER was almost deserted. Under the woodsy sign, *Elkhorn Cafe*, was a dusty pair of mule-deer antlers and a half-dozen tables with molded plastic chairs on wrought-iron legs. Kierra, wide-eyed though silent, seemed to take in everything from her perch in the infant seat, which Eleanor had set at the back of their table, securing it against the knotty pine wall behind.

A slim girl with straight blonde hair and an appealing friendly face, set water and menus before them. "The chili's good but there isn't much of it left. Rusty made a pot of French onion soup, too."

Eleanor ordered orange juice and coffee and Jim decided on a mountainburger, the eating of which proved to be a full-time job. He talked around mouthfuls of thick hamburger, dripping cheese, and juicy tomatoes. "I still can't get over the baby, Ellie. I wouldn't have believed this much improvement was possible in so short a time. I'm going to do a paper on her, so I hope you're keeping the kind of notes I need." He dipped a steaming French fry in a small pool of yellow mustard.

"I have been. Every day there's change. It's really exciting, Jim. She's a wonderful baby. I'm certain that not only is she basically normal, she's also very bright." She sipped the coffee and basked in the pleasure of being assured she was doing a good job. This was one area of great rapport between them; talking shop. Jim had watched her feed, bathe, and change the baby, and he had given her a careful examination as well.

"It's amazing. Have you discovered the causes of her former neglect?" He removed a slice of onion from his sandwich and took another bite.

Eleanor was silent. Then she shrugged. "I think the mother is resentful and gave the child less than minimal attention. I can feel a lot of resentment over the baby from everyone in the house, and I mean everyone! I don't know why. I haven't really had a personal chance to observe anyone with Kierra. No one other than her father seems the slightest interested in the baby. No one comes. Never." She was still not reconciled with that fact. The infant should have been a focal point of happiness in the family, and yet she was shunned by all. *Even Michael himself still treats her like a strange blossom he's somehow found in his garden and doesn't quite know how to identify. A flower or a weed?* she asked herself unhappily. She reached out and patted the child's soft hand protectively. The big blue eyes turned to her with placid beauty. Eleanor felt her heart ache.

"Ellie, I have to talk to you. You've been on my

mind since you left. I got Kal Wineburg to take over today so that I could see you." He glanced at his watch, then pushed his empty plate back. "I do have to make my hospital rounds later, though."

The cafe door opened and a stream of laughing people strolled in shouting greetings to the blonde girl. Two little girls, one very blonde, the other with dark red hair, tumbled through the door, shrieking as they raced to embrace the waitress. "Hi, Patti!"

Jim smiled at the newcomers, then shook his head. "Come on, let's get out of here or we'll have to scream to hear each other." He fumbled with his wallet and left a bill on the table. "Last of the big spenders. Come on."

Eleanor glanced at the money with some surprise. She knew the doctor had to be in an excellent mood to leave such a tip.

The Porsche sped them up the road, but they drove on past the gates to Bloodstone. "What's up ahead?"

"Campgrounds. At the end of the road is a place to park where the falls are."

He found the area and since they were alone he expansively filled two parking slots with his small car. The baby was secure and half asleep in her niche in the well behind the bucket seats.

"Ellie, I'm going to come right to the point," he said, turning toward her without so much as a glance at the falls. He looked very handsome and confident in his brown leisure suit, his pale hair slightly mussed by the wind. "I've missed you, Ellie. We've played games long enough. I'm in love with you. You know that." He waited for her reaction.

She was silent, waiting for her emotions to tell her what to say or do. She felt only a sense of calm. *It isn't that I don't feel the old attraction to him or that his words don't feel good, but something's missing, something's missing ... something terribly important. Maybe it always was!* With a sensation of sadness she found herself thinking not of the handsome doctor by her side but of Michael Matthews.

When she didn't respond, he began again. "You should be having babies of your own, not taking care of other people's children. You should be taking care of our children."

Her surprise showed in her large brown eyes. "Have you forgotten that you're married, Jim?"

His eyes were steady on hers. "I've done a lot of thinking lately, Ellie. I want to marry you. I'll divorce Jean."

His words stunned her, yet on another level they didn't seem to touch her at all. She held his gaze and fought off a wave of sadness while self-realization made everything come sharply into focus. While the man she believed herself to be in love with spoke words she had secretly longed to hear, she could only think of another man, one she had known a very short time, one she had no reason, no right, to love. The handsome historian's kind eyes, his deeply troubled face, filled her vision. "No, Jim, it won't work. You can't do that to Jean or the children. Or to yourself, either."

He shook his head. "I can't *not* do this, Ellie. Not if you love me." He took her hand.

"Don't let missing me confuse you, Jim. Please. I ... I think we both knew it was time for me to leave." Her fingers felt limp in his hand. *He's offering me what I wanted so badly ... now I don't want it. ...*

"Are you telling me you don't love me?" He looked

away from her, to his hands which were now both gripping the contoured steering wheel tightly. "Is that what you're saying?"

She sighed. "I don't know how I feel about you," she said truthfully. "I only know I have to stay where I am right now."

He looked at her measuringly. Finally he, too, sighed. "All right. But think about it, Ellie. Call me if you change your mind. Promise?"

She nodded through a film of tears. *What a fool I've been! How could I allow myself to love him when there's so much I don't know!* She felt a sudden desire to pack her things and run.

He suddenly snapped his fingers, startling her. "How could I almost forget? Millicent Judson is close to the end. She's at home, and though I have a nurse—Lisa—she's insistent on seeing you. I promised I'd ask you to come."

"Oh, no!" Millicent Judson was Eleanor's favorite patient, a cantankerous, energetic old woman with a heart several sizes larger than her body. She had been slowly dying of the cancer nibbling at her organs for all the time Eleanor had known her, and her plucky attitude and constant though salty humor had won Millicent a special place in the nurse's heart. Although she had always known death was inevitable, Eleanor couldn't help the sudden lump that formed in her throat. "How soon?"

Jim shrugged. "I don't give her much more than a few days, Ellie. She's out of it most of the time and I've instructed Lisa to keep her out of pain as much as possible." He took her hand. "Can you arrange something about the baby and stay with her? I won't swear she'll know you're there, at least not all of the time, but. . . ."

82

Eleanor nodded. Whatever Jim's faults, she knew him to be a compassionate doctor who shared her frustration when their combined skills could do nothing more than learn to accept what had to be.

"Of course. I hate to leave Kierra at this stage, but. . . ." she thought desperately of possibilities. Mrs. Sanchez was out. She considered the son. In the end, she had Jim take her to the mansion where she appealed to the baby's mother. Catherine, who was having a drink in the library, agreed with obvious irritation to watch the infant in Eleanor's absence. The nurse left formula and careful, tactful instructions. But when she hurried to the car with her overnight bag she was crying. She almost changed her mind and let Jim go without her, but the image of old Mrs. Judson dying alone was equally dismaying.

* * *

Three evenings later, after standing by until the frail lifeless body of her friend had been taken away by the morticians, Eleanor again entered Bloodstone. It was just beginning to darken, and the nurse moved heavily to the kitchen door which was the nearest entrance from where Lisa, the other nurse, had dropped her off. She felt a twinge of sadness that Millicent Judson had died and she vowed that some of the old woman's courage and wisdom would be absorbed into her own life.

The kitchen was softly lit and empty, though the oven was on and a great pot bubbled slowly on the stove. She pushed through the door. Immediately she heard the voices. They were raised in anger. She stood still, not wanting to hear but afraid to proceed and be discovered listening.

"How much more proof do you need? What kind of a man are you anyway?" The dry voice of Lucas Matthews bellowed through the house. "She's with him every chance she gets! We destroy him and his damned saloon! Do you hear me? By God, boy, if it was my woman, I'd be rid of them both!"

His grandson's voice was muffled.

"If you were half a man you'd get vengeance! Can't you understand that! I'd destroy them, bone by bone."

At once all that Eleanor had not understood on their walk through the forest earlier that week was vividly clear. More than land between Bloodstone and the saloon . . . there was a woman. *It was Ken Fletcher on the phone with Catherine that day of the storm! Ken Fletcher is Catherine Matthews' lover!*

Quietly Eleanor let herself out through the kitchen door. When she entered through the main entrance she knocked very loudly. Ricardo Sanchez opened the door, his dark face impassive. Only soft music could be heard in the background. No one else was in sight. "Ah, pretty nurse! Welcome home."

CHAPTER SEVEN

ELEANOR AWAKENED GROGGILY, feeling aches in every joint of her body. Her head throbbed less than when she had gone to sleep, but it still pounded softly. Seeing Kierra had affected her like receiving a physical blow. Even after hours of sleep she was still weak with helpless rage at what she had found.

Kierra had been in her crib, sleepless, her wide staring eyes pinned on the blank ceiling. She appeared to have shriveled considerably in the three days. Her hair was matted and her body red with prickly heat and a fiery resurgence of diaper rash. She turned empty eyes to Eleanor and the nurse half expected to see an expression of reproach in them. But they were like the eyes of a doll, glassy and vacant, withdrawing into a world only she could see.

Eleanor had scooped up the child and held her to her body, anger fighting with grief. Tears slid from her closed eyes. "My poor baby. What did she do with you?"

Then her professional training took over, momentarily relegating her emotions to the back seat. She bathed the baby and carefully creamed her entire body with the proper medications, then put her into a clean diaper. The baby refused to have anything to do with the solid food Eleanor prepared, even the ripe bananas, her favorite meal. She fought the bottle at first also, but when Eleanor persisted the child gave in. Soon she was nursing insatiably. Feeling sick inside, Eleanor knew that she was back at first base. Only now she was dealing with a child who had even less reason than ever to trust. She thought of Catherine Matthews, feeling she could coldly kill the woman at that moment for what she had done to her helpless baby. It was an emotion the nurse had never experienced before, an anathema to her chosen profession.

But I'm the one to blame! she told herself. *Whatever the need outside the house, I should not have abandoned the child. I should have hired another nurse and paid for her out of my own pocket rather than give the baby up to people who had already proven their . . . their criminal inadequacy!* Again she looked in at herself and found reason to despair. Once again she had neglected professional objectivity in a rush of emotion. She had thought of the old woman dying alone, without someone who cared deeply, and she had allowed Kierra to step back into the hell out of which she had barely begun to climb.

She cradled the baby in her arms and allowed the tears to flow freely, recriminating herself and giving in to a rare moment of unabashed hatred for the cruelty in others. The child's father crossed her mind, driving the stake farther into her heart.

Where was he these last few days? Why did I assume that nothing so terrible could happen to Kierra with Michael here? Have I been lying to myself? Has love made me that much of a fool?

During the quiet times at Millicent's bedside, she'd had time to think. Jim's proposal had brought it all to the surface of her mind, and while the old woman dozed there was finally time to think. She knew she had rejected Jim's offer not because of his wife and children but because she was in love with Michael Matthews. There was no way to explain or justify that love. It was there to be endured. She could expect nothing of it other than the very pain she had come to Bloodstone to avoid. She was powerless to explain or change that joyless love. She had considered putting distance between herself and Michael but she couldn't bear the thought of leaving Kierra. Now that she had come home and seen the infant she knew she never had the option at all. She couldn't leave the child now, whatever the cost to herself. Not until all the mysteries were sorted out. Not until she could walk away from the child with no fear for her safety. *I have to stay, now. I have to place myself between the baby and the world.* She knew she would fight like a desperate animal to keep Kierra safe. If she abandoned the baby to her world—in this case to her own family— she had no doubt that the child would be dead in months. Eleanor knew that she would rather die herself than let such a thing happen.

She rocked the child in the darkening room, inhaling the now-familiar scent of old perfume, clean baby flesh, the faintly medicinal odor of ointment, and she tasted her own hot salty tears. *I'll never leave you again, sweetheart. I promise, baby. I'll never let this happen again.*

She had gotten the baby to sleep and regained a semblance of composure when the door opened and Catherine Matthews, looking beautiful in a white hostess gown, appeared in the doorway. "Oh, I hadn't realized you were back! How wonderful. I was just about to leave." Her eyes flickered coldly over the sleeping child in the crib. "I'll say good night, then." She sipped from a glass in her hand and smiled impersonally, showing her deep dimples to advantage.

The desire to strike the woman across her exquisite face was almost overwhelming. Eleanor's fists tightened into hard balls and she had to force her breath to steady as the door closed behind the child's mother. She knew that if she gave in to the urge to attack the woman even on a verbal level only she and Kierra would lose. She would be forced to leave, and she would have to relinquish the child to her tormentors. She remembered the gutsy old woman who had died in her arms hours before and let the door close silently behind Catherine. She would be calm, and in the end she would win. *More important, Kierra would win!*

Sleep had been a long time coming. Even after she could cry no more, Eleanor still sobbed quietly into her pillow. Then, sleepless, feeling as if she had undergone a physical beating, she got up and made a thick paste of cereal and fruit and thinned it with milk. She laced it generously with vitamin drops, then gently awakened the baby and coaxed her into taking an extra meal. Warm and foggy with sleep, the little child accepted the wide-holed nipple without resistance, sucking until the bottle was almost empty. Satisfied, Eleanor put the infant back to sleep and finally was able to close her own eyes.

She awakened unsure of what had disturbed her slumber, and immediately dragged her aching body to the nursery. The baby was still sleeping quietly. It was as she was tugging the comforter up over the baby's frail shoulders that she heard the muffled arguing. It was faint and distant, but the anger seeped through the thick walls and seemed to fill the room with its vibration. Silently she went to the door. The voices became much louder but still beneath the level of comprehension.

Eleanor found her robe and slippers and put them on. She went out into the hall, wondering what had prompted such anger in the middle of the night. She was sure it was Michael and Lucas again. Part of her wanted to steal back to bed and escape in sleep, but something compelled her to take advantage of every opportunity to find out what was going on at Bloodstone. She told herself that Kierra's very life might be at stake.

"She's with him now, you fool!" Lucas' voice thundered up the stairs, every word an arrow that hit its mark with sickening clarity. "Go see for yourself!"

Eleanor's heart thudded in her chest, and the next thing she heard was the violent slamming of the massive front door. A moment later she heard the heavy-footed sound of Lucas stomping off to his library.

She returned to her bed but knew sleep was impossible. The whole house seemed to reek of violence and danger. She closed her eyes and the psychic smell only intensified. *Something's going to happen here*, she thought painfully, remembering the way she had felt that day on the patio with the family. *Something terrible is going to happen, and there's no way I can stop any of it!* She grasped her pillow and hugged it to her. All she could think of was Michael out there in the dark on his way to the saloon for a confrontation with the saloon's owner and Catherine. She was filled with apprehension, with fear for him. *It's not my business*, she told herself frantically. *It's not for me to care! I have only the baby to think of!*

She threw the pillow to the floor and reached blindly for her clothing. She was dressed in seconds, and with her shoes in her hand slipped down the great stairs and outside through the kitchen exit. She took a moment to put on her shoes, then began to run as quietly as she could down the path. Her mind seemed unusually clear, as clear as the midnight air, sparkling with as many thoughts as the black velvet sky was studded with jewel-like stars.

She took the path she had walked with Michael, stumbling in the dark, grateful to the sliver of moon and the vividness of the stars. The milky way was a boulevard of illumination, and she picked her way over obstacles. She had no idea what she'd say to Michael if she reached him before he arrived at the saloon. She only knew that something was going to happen, something terrible, and she knew she had to see the terrible thing did not happen to him.

Tireless, she turned first to the wrong path, then discovered her error and found the right one. She hurried past the place where she had seen the spider and the butterfly, past the fallen tree, and finally past the point where she and Michael had turned back to the house.

From quite a distance Eleanor could see the faint glow of the lights from the saloon. She followed the light, taking just enough care to keep herself from tripping and therefore traveling at less than a run. *He had too great a head start while I deliberated and then dressed! He would have reached the saloon long before now.*

The path veered to the left and opened to the main road. She ran lightly through the trees at the edge of the compound, hearing music and an assortment of loud voices. It sounded like a party, but as she came closer the sound of a woman's laughter rang out, shrill and evil and close to where Eleanor stood. She leaned against a tree and caught her breath.

The parking lot had only a few cars in it. The closest, parked away from the others, was a small blue sportscar. Its motor was racing impatiently and Eleanor could barely make out the outline of a young man sitting at the wheel. Caught in the reflected light next to him was Catherine Matthews, and it was she from whom the laughing originated. Even from the distance Eleanor could see that the woman was very drunk, and from the raucous laughter from the driver, he had matched her drink for drink. Alongside the car, his shoulders slumped, his fists balled but hanging at his sides, Michael Matthews stood by impotently. With a great roar, the car lurched forward and skidded onto the road, then raced down the mountain, a trail of dust, pebbles, and screeching laughter in its wake. Mocked and ridiculed, his eyes fastened on the winding road which ate the taillights of the sports car, the historian stood quietly while Eleanor watched.

Her heart one mass of pain for him, Eleanor

turned from the man she loved. She knew that he must not see her at so naked, so shameful a moment. *He might never again be able to meet my eyes.* She retraced her steps woodenly, moving fast enough so that she would be home before him. Yet she paused breathlessly as she reached the giant rocks behind the house. The moon touched them with its slender finger, and where it touched the rocks bled. She stood very very still, knowing that something even more terrible was yet to come. . . .

CHAPTER EIGHT

THE NIGHT WAS endless. From her bed she saw the sightless eyes of the stars staring back at her with unblinking patience. She had undressed mechanically and positioned herself on her bed, at a loss with what to do with time, with herself . . . the hurt that was in her, extending from her heart to Kierra to Michael and back to herself. Finally she settled for mindlessly tossing and turning on the bed, concentrating only on the stars, the wrinkles in the sheets, the way her long hair tangled against her neck as she twisted her head from side to side.

From a long way off, the phone rang and echoed through the house. She listened to it dully, one part of her tired mind aware that the phone should not be ringing in the dead of night, the other part quietly accepting, waiting, knowing that this was still another act in the drama she had been expecting from the time she had first come to this house. She heard the voice of a maid, then the voice of a man. She listened to the silence and then to the flurry of feet. She felt the excitement suddenly in the air. Still she didn't move. The phone rang again, was this time quickly answered, and later, rang still another time. The first powdering of morning slipped over the sky, sucking from it one layer of darkness.

With a weary sigh, knowing what had happened was a reality and that there was no escaping from it, she rose from the bed and put on her robe. She stepped into her slippers and opened her door. She blinked in the softly lighted hallway, then turned toward the staircase and nearly collided with Mrs. Sanchez.

"Ooh!" The older woman quickly steadied her hand which held a full mug of steaming milk. "It is for *señor* Matthews. He is upset. He must sleep," she said with confusion. Then, her eyes seemingly focusing on the nurse for the first time, her voice steadied. "Oh, Miss Lawrence!"

"What is it? What's happened?"

The Mexican woman shook her head. "It is Mrs. Matthews. There has been an accident. She and the man who owns the saloon were driving down the road—"

"What has happened?" Eleanor interrupted impatiently, her fear taking control. "Dr. Matthews. . . . Is . . . is he all right?"

"Dr. Matthews?" she asked with confusion. "*Sí*, he is fine. It is not Mr. Michael. . . ." The veil of confusion lifted and the women looked at each other. The older woman nodded slightly, her intelligent eyes registering enlightenment. For the briefest of instances they shared perfect understanding. "He is well, miss."

Eleanor broke the spell. "Yes? What is it?" She took a deep breath. "Is she dead?"

Teresa Sanchez nodded slowly. "Yes, she is dead. There was an accident. The car . . . I do not know. She is dead."

"And the driver?" she asked, thinking of the shadow who had laughed so cruelly from behind the wheel.

The Mexican woman's eyes clouded briefly. "No, I am told that the Fletcher man is not badly injured. Mrs. Matthews, she was thrown from the car, under . . . under the wheels."

Eleanor nodded, strangely calm now that the terrible thing had finally happened. "Where is Dr. Matthews?"

She looked down at the cooling mug. "I must take this to Mr. Matthews." She looked toward the stairs. "He is downstairs in the library. Waiting for the coroner." She hurried past the younger woman and tapped softly at the door to the old man's room.

Eleanor hurried down the steps, but as she neared the library she grew timid. She had dealt with death many times in her life as a nurse, and in her private world. But she had no words for Michael about his wife. Yet she wanted to be with him, if only so that he would not have to be alone.

"Michael?" In spite of his wishes, it was the first time she had ever called him by his first name.

He looked up from a letter he was writing, and his eyes, which were shot through with blood, turned slowly to her face. "Eleanor. Did someone awaken you?" His voice was very tired and very clear.

She shook her head. He was still wearing the dark slacks and white shirt he had been wearing when he went to the saloon. The jacket to his suit was behind his chair. He stood and slowly put it on. "I heard you were away for a few days. I didn't know. I had to go to San Francisco on business." He gestured toward an overstuffed leather chair. "Please."

It felt as if a great weight was lifted from her shoulders. *He wasn't home! He didn't have anything to do with Kierra's treatment! He doesn't even know about it!* She could handle anything from Michael but cruelty toward his own child.

"You know . . . about Catherine?"

She nodded, then sank into the chair near him. "I . . . I'm sorry," she said, knowing that she did feel sorrow, though not for the dead woman.

He sat down and shook his head slowly. "I am, too, but not so much that she's dead as that she never really had a chance to live. I blame myself for that." He spoke with a minimum of emotion, yet the pain was etched in his grave face.

Eleanor didn't know how to respond. From what she had observed, Catherine Matthews was intent only on having her own life, regardless of the cost to anyone else.

As if reading her mind, Michael shrugged. "You don't understand. I mean her drinking, for one thing. I should have been stronger. I should have helped her, not let her go on as she was." He looked up and met her eyes. "I should have cared more." He shook his head. "I sent her to Fletcher, in my own way. I did that to her, too."

Eleanor spoke very gently. "I've worked with alcoholics professionally, Michael, and there's really little anyone can do for them if they resist change. It's a very personal choice."

He nodded, then shook his head again. "My guilt

is greater, Eleanor. I married Catherine knowing what she was, with no real intention of helping her, of giving her anything more than my name, my money. . . . I married her because she was beautiful and looking at her lifted my depression. I married her because I thought I would feel less alone. I never gave her anything of value."

"You gave her a child," Eleanor said softly. She was unprepared for his bitter, agonized laughter.

"Oh, yes. That." He waved his hand as if to erase the thought from existence. "Don't misunderstand, Eleanor. I'm not putting myself through pain because of what happened. Ours was not a good marriage, as I know you know. And I'm not even mourning a woman I could not love, a woman who despised me. I'm not even mourning the loss of a mother for Kierra, because I know what kind of a mother she was. I *am* mourning, though. I'm mourning a life never led, a marriage never begun. I'm mourning a very beautiful girl who was brought up to barter that beauty for a comfortable bed, a pretty gift. I knew who and what my wife was, Eleanor, and I did nothing to change her. I just tried to use her to keep from loneliness. And it didn't even work." He looked down at the shot glass of whiskey on the side table. He reached for it, had second thoughts, and left it where it was.

Eleanor felt an urgency to speak. She reached out impulsively and touched his hand. "But that's not fair, Michael! We all grasp for people to chase away our loneliness. That's how we tell ourselves we're in love, when we find something in someone else that makes us feel happier with us. At one time Catherine made you happy. That's why you wanted to be with her, to marry her. Maybe the kind of happiness she gave you wasn't the kind that lasted, and maybe what you offered in return wasn't enough. But you weren't wrong, not in the beginning. Neither of you. Later . . . maybe it was the baby, or habit, or because you made the commitment, I don't know . . . but maybe then it was the time to admit it was over, or whatever, and go separate ways. But it wasn't wrong to reach out for what you each thought was right, then. Maybe. . . ." She couldn't resist a tender smile. "Maybe you just stayed too long at the fair."

He stared at her blankly, then the same soft, wondering smile touched the corners of his sculptured mouth. He started to speak then thought better of it.

Her hand on his felt alive a thousandfold over. She trembled where their flesh met, and she knew that he was feeling the same shock. The love Eleanor felt expanded as she sat there, and she knew that at this moment when Michael might have been at his lowest ebb, he too was riding the dazzling crest of the same irrepressible hapiness she felt. The words threatened to spill from her lips. *Oh, Michael, I love you. . . .* He opened his mouth to speak.

Distantly she was aware of someone at the main door. Mrs. Sanchez, now dressed, was ushering two people toward the library. But it was not until they actually entered the room that Eleanor withdrew her hand and looked away from the man she loved.

Eleanor greeted the coroner and Norma Vanowen briefly, then excused herself and went to her room. As she climbed the stairway she had the strangest feeling that someone somewhere had just lowered a curtain and called out a new act. . . .

CHAPTER NINE

THE HEAVENS, ASSUMING a proper funeral air, drew clouds together in a tight circlet of gray that crowned a slate-colored sky. Another summer storm threatened on the horizon, and from a long way off the faint flash of lightning illuminated an otherwise darkening forest.

Eleanor zipped the side of her only good black dress and slid her nyloned feet into the slim black pumps which, after two years, still looked brand new. She paused briefly in front of the mirror, taking stock of herself before turning to prepare the diaper bag with the baby's essentials. Her reflection was somber, neat and yet attractive. She stared back at the image of herself, a lump in her throat as she thought of the grim purpose of this primping. Ray's funeral was the last she had attended, and at the time she had vowed never to attend another. Now she was going to witness the interment of the wife of the man she loved.

After the bag was ready Eleanor realized that, characteristically, she was early. Since Kierra was still fast asleep in her crib, the nurse tried to sit and read. But the words refused to come into focus and restlessly she began to pace the ample room. Growing bored, she opened the door and stepped into the hallway, once again enjoying the movie-theater atmosphere of dim lights, ornate wallpaper, and plush carpeting. She made her way slowly to the fish tanks at the top of the stairs, intending to lose herself in their watery depths until it was time to get Kierra ready. She didn't want to think about the funeral ahead, nor did she want to involve herself any more than absolutely essential with the family or Catherine's relatives who would soon arrive. She wanted to be with Michael and help him in any way she could, but he was being swallowed up in details, in the paperwork and procedure of death.

A slender zebra fish shot across the coral landscape after its mate as Eleanor bent to observe the watery life within the tank. Immediately she heard the voices from the hall below, and again she was powerless to do anything other than listen. She was growing somewhat used to the battle between Lucas Matthews and his grandson, but she was surprised to hear their raised voices on the day of Catherine's funeral. Now that the red-haired beauty was dead, Eleanor found herself wondering what it was they could be arguing about.

"Are you a fool, boy? Where's my cigarettes?"

Eleanor sat by the tank during the pause that followed. Then she heard Lucas' hacking cough. His voice was strained, but the volume was as loud as before. "Don't be a fool, Michael! Get out of it while you can! While there's still time!"

Michael's voice fought to stay calm and controlled. The effort it took was reflected in each word. "I don't want to talk about it, Grandfather. Forget it."

Again the cough. "Fool," he hissed. "They'll be here any minute! Now is the time to speak your piece. Or I will!"

"Grandfather, I forbid you to speak to them!" Michael's voice rose.

"You forbid!" It was the roar of a wounded bull. The cough seemed muted in comparison. "Damn your forbid! I say let them take the child!"

Eleanor sat up.

"Let them have her! This might be your only chance. Damn it, son, don't you understand? Give her to them now!" Lucas Matthews' voice was an evil rasp. "Don't be a damn fool. Don't be more a fool than you've already been!"

"Keep out of this, old man!"

Eleanor flinched at the degree of unadulterated hatred in Michael's tone.

"Keep out of my life. Keep out of my child's life!"

The laugh that filled the stairwell and rose to the lighted fish tanks was loud and humorless. "*Your* child!" He started to laugh again, but stopped himself just before his next fit of racking coughs began.

"Look, let's drop it, okay?" Michael once again fought for calmness. "I have some work to do before the others arrive."

Eleanor bit down on her bottom lip and waited, sensing that more was to come. She felt a tightness in her muscles as she strained to hear through the silence, and she knew somehow that on this, the morning of Catherine's funeral, she would find out what it was that kept Kierra apart from these men who should have loved her without measure.

"The work can wait," Lucas said finally.

"Grandfather," Michael began warningly, his voice edgy and cold.

"The work can wait! I'm telling you . . . I'm begging you . . . not to take on the raising of Catherine's child! I won't have it, damn it! I won't be forced to live in the same house with—"

"Grandfather!"

"No, damn it, boy! This is too important! I won't let you deny it! First I'm deprived of my land by Fletcher, and now, if you're given your hand, I'm to be forced to live in the same house with his. . . ."

"Grandfather!" It was more a cry than a word.

". . . Bastard!"

The word thundered through the hallways and into Eleanor's stunned brain. She pressed her palm against the glass of the tank, grateful for its solid reality. Blood roared in her ears as the word echoed through her mind.

"She could be mine!"

Eleanor steadied herself as Michael's protest reached her prison on the second floor. She waited for the old man to speak, fearing and yet expecting his cruel, cutting laugh. Instead, his voice when it came was unexpectedly soft and tinged with sorrow.

"Don't be a fool. She was with him all the time. We both know it. The child is his. You must send her away. Catherine's people will raise her. The duty is theirs, not ours."

"She could be my child, Grandfather," Michael insisted softly. "You don't know she isn't. Nor do I."

The old man's voice rose and firmed. "Stop fooling yourself, boy. She's his. More, there's something wrong with you, you can see that, can't you? Do you want to be saddled with that, Michael? Let them take her! I'll talk to them." His voice dropped and became wheedling, pursuasive. "You won't have to speak at all. I'll take them aside and talk to them, and they'll take her away. You'll marry again, and far better, and you'll bring children to this house who belong here! Don't be a fool!"

"She could be mine," the younger man insisted stubbornly.

"All right! Have it your way! Be blind to the truth! I offer you a decent chance to be free, and you talk dreams and deceive yourself! But mark my words, boy, you'll live to regret it! Raise the bastard of that man and you'll live to see me kill him!"

After a long thick silence, Michael's voice, soft once again, rose on the tension-filled air. "Kierra is my daughter. She'll be raised as my daughter. With love and respect. I'll see to it. There's no need for killing unless someone can prove to me that she's not my daughter. If there was a need for killing I'd do it with my own hands. Don't protect me, Grandfather. Just help me to love the child."

Lucas Matthews began to speak after a long moment. "You would have me. . . ."

The doorbell rang loudly, and a second later subdued voices echoed through the hallway from the front door.

Eleanor remained where she was until she heard the two men move away and toward their company. Then, knees shaking, she got up and began to make her way back to the nursery, to her charge.

A thought, far from consoling but definitely enlightening, came to her mind. *At least and at last, she told herself dryly, I finally know what's "wrong" with Kierra.* Aching with love and pity, she roused the sleeping child and took her into her arms.

CHAPTER TEN

THE FUNERAL PROVED to be considerably less painful than Eleanor had anticipated. There was a short eulogy delivered by a minister. The closed coffin was covered over with a large spray of pale pink roses. At Michael's request the service was private and simple.

Before she knew it, Eleanor found herself back in the limousine on her way to the estate again. She patiently endured the mingled "oohs" and "aahs" of relatives who had never seen Kierra before, then was able to excuse herself and the baby on the grounds that the infant needed lunch and her nap.

She buried herself in crocheting a toy panda bear from a rather elaborate pattern while the baby slept, refusing to think of anything other than the work at hand. But a collage of funerals stole across her mind, starting with her father's and stopping with Ray's. She added an extra row of black by mistake and had to rip it out.

When the baby woke up, she gave her a bath, coaxing Kierra into enjoying the tepid water and the slippery feel of the soap. The child's response to her care was gratifying. Her big blue eyes followed the young nurse everywhere, and one baby hand clutched the yellow duck even while she bathed.

The rest of the afternoon threatened to crawl, and when Mrs. Sanchez appeared at her door with a request that she join the extended family for dinner, the girl was quick to reject the offer on the grounds that Kierra was fussy over a tooth that was coming through. In spite of her loneliness, Eleanor wanted to keep far away from everyone connected with Catherine Matthews until she had time to sort out her feelings and calm her nerves. She recalled Lucas' threat to kill the supposed father of her ward. Eleanor realized that the old man had meant every word. She found herself stealing quick glances at the baby, searching hard for signs of identity, looking for some hint of the Matthews' features on the innocent face of the infant.

She sang to the baby as she put her to sleep for the night, smiling down at the full, contented child whose eyes followed her everywhere. She hummed a lullaby and watched the eyes slowly close, her own stinging with unshed tears. She felt pity for the child that would have to grow up without a mother, in spite of her knowledge of what kind of a mother Catherine had been. But in the private sanctuary of her hidden thoughts, Eleanor mourned not only for the child without a mother, but for a child who likely had no father, as well. She prayed that Michael was strong enough to withstand the pressure and hatred from his grandfather, and that somehow, perhaps with her help, he could find a place in his heart for the precious little girl in the crib. She remembered his question to her on the patio that day, when he had asked, *What is a father?*

She answered him with her mind, with her heart, into the total silence of the night. *A father is love. A father is caring. A father is the man who takes the responsibility. It's so much more than a biological function!* Yet she knew that no logic on earth could coax so important a response as love. He would either learn to sincerely love and accept the child, or Kierra would grow like a sunless flower, weak and pale and so terribly alone.

She bathed in the bathroom that adjoined her room, relaxing finally in the tub of hot water scented with violet essence. Her thoughts drifted to Michael, as they did so often, and she longed for some way to lighten his burden of guilt. She knew that it was his sense of failure that made him want to accept the responsibility of raising Catherine's child. But she knew that the failure of their marriage didn't belong on his shoulders alone. She was wise enough to understand that acceptance had to come from within, and that she was powerless to do more than stand by him and offer her love and support. She would also work with the child he had at least verbally accepted. Lucas Matthews' words stung as she remembered his rejection of Kierra on the grounds that there was something innately wrong with the child. That she could and would do for Michael as well as for Kierra herself—she would grow to be a normal, happy, enchanting child under Eleanor's loving hand. She would—someday—win even the old man over completely.

On that pleasant fairy tale, Eleanor got out of the bath. She put on a freshly laundered gown and robe, did her nails, and brushed her long glossy hair. She snapped on the small radio by her bed and fumbled with the dials until she had located some soft, sentimental music. It had been a long day but she was not tired. Tomorrow the relatives would be gone, and hopefully life would return to some semblance of normalcy—*if anything at Bloodstone could be called normal,* she added to herself. She turned off the overhead light and the gentle illumination of the bedside lamp with its rose-colored shade cast shadows over the room. She liked her room and the house itself, yet she shuddered. *That's what this is,* she thought, *a house of shadows, stained with blood and tragedy and deep, dark secrets. . . .*

She jumped at the sound of soft tapping at her door. Teresa Sanchez looked very small as she stood in the doorway wrapped in a long black shawl. Her eyes darted around furtively as Eleanor opened the door and then, without waiting to be asked, she stepped into the room and shut the door quietly behind her.

"Yes?" Eleanor looked at the servant curiously and with the same aura of distaste she'd felt since witnessing the destruction of the butterfly.

The dark-haired woman glanced around the room suspiciously, then visibly relaxed when she realized they were alone except for the sleeping infant in the next room. "I have come to tell you that you must tell them that you cannot care for the child any longer." Her black eyes were shaded. "Tell them you must go away, that they will have to make other arrangements for the baby."

Eleanor looked at her wonderingly, momentarily

concerned that the strain of the accident and funeral had snapped the woman's hold on reality. "I . . .I don't understand."

Mrs. Sanchez shook her head impatiently. "*Sí*, you understand." Her expression was gentle, almost compassionate, the look of a woman who has borne the weight of responsibility for men for all of eternity. "This must stop before there is more bloodshed. Make them give her away! Without you they cannot keep the child, and once the child is out of this house perhaps the danger will be gone!"

Eleanor stared at her, only half understanding. "You mean that Lucas will stop at nothing to get the land he wants from Ken Fletcher, especially if he has to live in the same house with what he believes is the child of the man?" She had no reason now to suppose the servant knew anything less than the truth.

The older woman nodded quickly. "*Sí*. The blood will continue to rain down on this house unless you stop it! Let the child go! Then, perhaps, he will be appeased. She will be gone, and the mother buried deep in the earth."

For a long moment the two women studied each other silently and motionlessly. As they had done in the hallway, each had total understanding of the other's hunger.

"You love him?" Eleanor asked finally, wanting to hear the words although she knew the answer.

"*Sí*. As you love the grandson, so I love him. As women we have to take matters upon ourselves. We must sacrifice the child to save the man. Lucas Matthews cannot live with the shame of the child. He will kill her father to avenge his disgrace, or Michael will have to kill him to stop Lucas. Or kill his own grandfather! But all day I think, and I realize you hold the power to stop all this. Go away! Give them no choice but to give up the infant. You can return later, you can get what you want. He is a good man, Michael. He will love you. Later you will have children of your own. Please, I beg this of you!"

Eleanor reached out and grasped the arm of a chair to steady herself. She looked at the other woman with horror. "There's no one who will love Kierra! None of them will be able to take care of her, nurse her back to health! You don't know what you're asking. I can't do anything to induce them to send the baby away as if she were an . . . an animal!"

The wise tireless eyes of the Mexican woman burned with the same steady intensity. "*Sí*, if she were an animal I would put her in the grave along with her bitch mother myself! This I would do for him." She paused. "And this is what you must do if you love Michael. There is time in the morning to make your announcement. I will leave you now to think, and I will be waiting."

Eleanor thought she heard a subtle threat in the woman's final words. Silently she watched the servant leave the room. When the door was firmly shut against her, Eleanor walked slowly to the adjoining nursery. The dim light from her bedside lamp barely reached into the room, but she could easily make out the pink velvety-skinned face of her charge. The little lashes curved low over the rounded cheekbones, and the tiny rosebud mouth moved ever so slightly, nursing the air as she slept.

Eleanor studied the little face she knew and loved so well, and a separate, logical side of her observed the child from a safe distance. First she wondered, with that cool part of herself, if there was truth to

Teresa Sanchez' appraisal of what would happen at Bloodstone if Kierra were to remain at the estate. She recalled the argument she had overheard the day before as she stood by the fish tank. Grudgingly she had to admit that Lucas Matthews might well be capable of killing Ken Fletcher for vengeance, for an act which he truly believed against his grandson, himself and his house.

She forced herself to follow the train of thought the other way. She imagined herself announcing some drastic need which would preclude her staying on at the estate to care for the child. She toyed with the possibility of Michael suggesting and obtaining another nurse. She finally concluded that in all likelihood he would be tempted to give into the demands of his grandfather. He hadn't been with Kierra long enough to have developed the genuine love which would override all concept of natural, biological fatherhood. He was torn with guilt, confusion, and pain, with his wife in her fresh grave. His emotions were ragged and uncertain. If she did as Mrs. Sanchez insisted, the child would leave with the relatives. She was suddenly sure of it.

Eleanor then appraised each person who was spending the night in the estate. She thought about Catherine's aunt and uncle who had raised her, but dismissed them at once. They were the reason that Catherine herself was the kind of person she had been. Under the words of concern and sorrow Eleanor had easily read disinterest and coldness. Never could she allow Kierra to go with them. She tried to be more liberal with Catherine's grandmother, a rather quiet old woman who seemed to genuinely grieve for the dead woman. Yet the old woman had barely smiled at the infant in all the time she'd been around her. No, she couldn't let the old woman care for the child, either.

All that was left was Catherine's sallow-faced sister, a widow with tremendous jowls and a face set permanently into an expression of disillusionment. Eleanor had talked to Janice briefly during the afternoon and found her a basically kind person. But life had disenchanted the young widow so severely that a child raised by her would accept defeat as she did the sun rising in the morning. *No, there's no one I could send Kierra to. Not for any reason! Not even to save Lucas, myself or even Michael! There must be another way!* she told herself, and she vowed to find it.

She was kissing the baby with heartfelt tenderness and still taking care not to disturb her slumber when again she heard a light tapping on her door. Steeling herself for another encounter with Mrs. Sanchez, she opened the door. "Michael!" she cried softly, stepping back to let him in.

He waited until she had closed the door behind him, then reached out and touched her cheek with his fingers. He dropped his hand immediately, as if burned by the contact.

"I . . . I hope you don't mind. I had to see you. It's been a long, long day, and I knew I'd go crazy if I didn't see you, talk to you, even for a minute. Were you asleep?"

She shook her head, then sat down on the small sofa, pointing to the matching armchair. She waited until he was seated, then searched his troubled face. He was very pale and looked older. "Oh, Michael! I wish there was something I could say. I know how difficult it's been." She wanted to say more but she didn't know how much he wanted her to know.

112

He gazed at her searchingly. "Yes. But it's almost over now. They'll all be gone tomorrow. I have to get back to my work. . . ." He shook his head. "Life will go on as before—my grandfather will try to own the world and that includes me. But you and the baby will be here and who knows, maybe the two of you will bring peace to this madhouse in time."

She heard the decision in his voice and knew that, whatever the price, she would go against the wishes of the housekeeper, doing everything in her power to bring father and daughter together. She would help create a bond between them. Her voice was patient and maternal. "I'll be here."

He got up and came to her, gently pulling the young nurse to her feet. "Look, Eleanor, I have no right. This is the wrong time. But I want to tell you that I . . . how I feel. I care about you. I want you to stay here. Your being here is what I lean on, what keeps me going when everything seems impossible. Promise me you'll stay."

She looked up and read the need and love in his eyes, praying that what he wanted wouldn't ultimately destroy him. "Of course I'll stay," she whispered, feeling the heat from his body.

"As long as you want me here."

His lips touched hers and for an instant all fear and sadness was drowned in the great crushing weight of her love for him. Then he was pulling away and grasping the handle of the door. "Until tomorrow," he breathed, disappearing into the hallway.

As if in a dream, the young woman made her way to her bed and sank beneath the covers. She touched slender fingers to the lips he had just kissed. As her eyes closed she felt hot tears slipping from between her lids. She thought of the decision she had made against the housekeeper's wishes, and knew suddenly that she was deeply obligated to offer some plan in return if she was to reject the one she had been offered.

She slept fitfully, dreaming in part of flowers and sunshine and a tall handsome man by her side. The rest was images of the hideous boulders that had given Bloodstone its name. The blood that oozed over them was the lifesap of the same young man of her happier dreams. The sheets under her slim body grew damp with perspiration, and finally, with the night still capping the sky, she awoke. She knew what she had to do. . . .

Lucas Matthews had a need for vengeance, a desire to even the score with the young owner of the saloon. But even more than he wanted retribution, Eleanor knew he wanted his land. If Kierra were to stay, then the same tranquilizing effect could be effected by the removal of Fletcher! With the saloon destroyed and the estate restored to its former size, Lucas would have fulfilled his greatest wish, and the need to avenge would disappear. Perhaps, with time and some effort, he might even come to accept the baby as his own great-grandchild, if he had his win against the man whom he assumed to be the child's biological father.

Excited, Eleanor went through the details in her mind, sure that she had come up with a plan that made far more sense than the one Teresa Sanchez had devised. She would have to find a way to persuade Ken Fletcher that with Catherine dead he should sell the land at a handsome profit and put an end to the senseless feud. She remembered what Michael had told her about the bogus land deal that

Norma was attempting to promote, and excitedly she saw it as a perfect avenue for achieving her ends. Fletcher would believe that Lucas Matthews would lose his land as well. Though not by nature a manipulative or deceptive person, she knew she would—and could—do whatever was necessary to put an end to the terrible battle between the men.

Having found something she could at least try in exchange for her inability to sacrifice Kierra, Eleanor closed her eyes and anticipated a dreamless rest. But her sleep proved to be a continuation of the worst of her former dreams. The thick blood continued to pour onto the rock. It drowned the earth and the trees and the small yellow flowers that grew between the blades of grass.

She awakened in a bath of icy perspiration as the blurred fingertips of dawn chased the night from the sky. *Something else*, she knew, *was going to happen....*

CHAPTER ELEVEN

ALTHOUGH BRIGHT AND sunny, the next day proved to be almost as difficult as the one past. A confusion in reservations caused Catherine's family to remain at the estate an extra day, further disrupting the routine of the household, and Kierra, whose first tooth was on the verge of breaking through, cried most of the day, would eat or drink nothing, and demanded Eleanor's full attention. By early afternoon she knew that there was little chance of seeing the saloon owner that day. Then came the weekend, when she surmised that business was heaviest, and grudgingly she resigned herself to postponing her talk until the following Monday.

She took her lunch on the patio with the family. Although there was some attempt at lightness, especially on the part of Norma Vanowen who had all but lived at the house since the accident, it was an uncomfortable meal. Eleanor was grateful for the excuse of Kierra's teething to disappear as quickly as possible.

At dinnertime the aunt and uncle insisted that Eleanor and Kierra join them at the table, in spite of Eleanor's suggestion that an ailing baby made a poor dinner companion. Mrs. Sanchez had prepared a lobster aspic arranged on crisp green lettuce cups, followed by cioppino, a full-bodied bouillabaisse stew of rich tomato sauce studded with white fish and seafood of every description. With it was crusty French bread and an excellent Caesar salad and wine. By the time the filet mignon arrived, Eleanor was more than full, and at dessert could only pick politely at the fresh strawberry tart with its creamy custard base.

The dinner conversation was determinedly cheerful, though laced with practical suggestions regarding various possessions that had belonged to Catherine. Michael was unusually silent throughout the entire meal, but his eyes frequently traveled the length of the table to Eleanor. The baby was subdued by the medicine the nurse had given her. She stared at the family, strangers to her, with large disapproving eyes as if she might at any second split the air with a very infantile scream. Eleanor was secretly pleased at the baby for her cautious behavior. *That's why you have to stay here with us* . . . she thought at her.

After dinner she took the baby to the nursery for one last attempt at a feeding. She wasn't overly concerned any longer because Kierra had been gaining weight steadily and was now almost at a normal weight. She wouldn't be hurt by skipping a meal since there was a good chance that she would make up for it the next day. Worn out by her tooth troubles, the baby was more than willing to leave food for the moment and escape into sleep. Eleanor, equally exhausted, took the same way out.

* * *

The weekend passed slowly once Catherine's family had departed. Michael locked himself in his study and Lucas Matthews took to his room. Mrs. Sanchez, save for reproachful glances from time to time, elected to leave the young nurse and her charge completely alone. Her son was a ghost, darting from one errand to the next. She waited up late Sunday night in hope that Michael might seek her out, but when the grandfather clock in the living room struck midnight she went to sleep.

Monday dragged interminably. Eleanor fed and bathed the baby, and by the time she was ready to go to the saloon, a call from Jim delayed her to the point that it was time to give Kierra her morning nap. She was impatient about the phone call, unhappy about being forced to rehash a love affair that was over before it had ever begun. She left the telephone depressed. Love seemed so easy for others and so painfully complex for her. She felt that Michael was beginning to love her, yet the mysteries and dangers of such a love frightened her. A part of her wished to find some way to disentangle herself with Bloodstone completely, leaving the complexities and problems for someone else to solve. But she knew she would go that very afternoon to the saloon to take an active role in the madness that persisted at the estate, and in doing so she would pledge her soul to Michael Matthews for all time , whatever else might happen . . . .

The clouds which had threatened to settle in again earlier evaporated by the time she set off down the path in the direction of the saloon. A lingering moistness in the air made the weather muggy as the sun rose in the sky. Eleanor wished she had worn lighter clothing, regretting her choice of Levi's and knit pullover. She paused to open the baby's coverall and push aside the lightweight blanket tucked around her. Trying to decide what tact to take with the saloon owner, her nervousness increased. She began to fear that the whole thing was futile, an empty gesture. *I, an absolute stranger, an employee at the Matthews' estate, am about to ask a man to close down his business and sell his land1! What can I possibly say to convince him?* she asked herself. Her steps faltered. Then she thought of Mrs. Sanchez and the baby. *There's got to be a way!*

The humidity intensified the odors of the forest as the sun baked down and lightly cooked the greenery. Summer wild flowers mingled their perfume with the fresh scent of pine needles, and the powdery fragrance of cedar wood fought the vanilla-extract smell of a nearby pine. Eleanor's fingers on the metal bar of the stroller were damp. She began to talk to the baby, attempting to cheer herself up by showing Kierra the beauty of the forest.

From the main road she could see the saloon area with its sturdy wooden slat fence and its dirt parking lot. There was only one car parked there, a blue Land Cruiser, and the rambling building looked closed, although the main entrance stood ajar, the sun pouring its beam into the darkness of the interior. As she came closer, she could see a man behind the car removing crates of food from the back seat. He was tall and wore a moustache, with curly dark hair and a slim, boyish body.

An old blue-green Chevrolet rounded the corner and slowed in front of the saloon. A man with leonine red hair and a beard to match leaned out the window. "Hey, Ken, man, I'll be a little late, okay?"

"Hold on there, Stash."

She walked more slowly, still too far away to make out the features of this man she had to find some way to reach. She watched as he walked over to the old car and talked to the powerfully built red-haired man. Womanlike, she wondered what had drawn Catherine Matthews to him and away from her husband. He appeared in casual good humor as he talked and laughed a moment with his friend. Eleanor wondered if he felt any grief or guilt over the young woman in her early grave.

The dark-haired young man waved a good-bye and turned back to his own car as the Chevy pulled off with a deep-throated roar. As he turned the sun caught him and he blinked. Nearby now, Eleanor stopped short, the breath leaving her lungs in a sudden rush as if she had been dealt a powerful blow. His full face was bathed in sunlight, each feature clear and distinct and completely recognizable. "Richard!" she cried out, her feet carrying her forward. "Richard!"

The young man looked up and squinted his eyes at the young woman wheeling the stroller down the road toward him. He took a step forward, hesitated, then began to move uncertainly toward the two of them. "Who? Ellie? God, is that you, Ellie?"

She didn't know whether to laugh or cry. In the

end she did neither. She reached him and was caught up in his embrace.

"I don't believe it! What are you doing here, little sister? How in hell did you find me?" He pushed her back slightly and looked at the baby. "And who's that?" He laughed suddenly. "Maybe you weren't looking for me. Maybe it's been longer than I thought."

She caught her breath and shook her head. "I was looking for Ken Fletcher, the saloon owner. I thought. . . ." A look of bewilderment passed across her pretty face as she remembered the red-haired man who had called her brother by another name.

He nodded. "That's me. Ken Fletcher." He laughed at her confusion. "Come on, let's go sit down and I'll get you something cold to drink and we'll talk. I own this place," he said with an expression of pride. "It's mine. Come on."

She let him lead her over to one of the picnic tables outside the saloon. He disappeared inside and returned with two frosted bottles of Coca-Cola. He glanced at the baby. "Yours?"

She shook her head. "I take care of her." She looked at him carefully. "You look good, Richard. Healthier."

He laughed. "Healthier, huh? Still the good little nurse, I see." He took a swig from his bottle. He made a face. "Be right back." He went into the building and when he returned he had an iced bottle of Coors in his hand. He drank and grinned.

Eleanor studied the face which resembled her own and felt a warmth as she remembered moments out of her childhood when they had been close. Then he had been her big brother, her protector and idol. She also saw the hardness that had crept into his face and heart in the years since then. She remembered the bitter fights . . . the money stolen from their mother's purse . . . the smashed geode. Hastily she discarded the bad memories and concentrated on the warmth of their earlier closeness, when their father was alive. "Well, tell me," she started and gestured toward the saloon and cabins, "about all this, I mean. And your name."

His face filled with the same mixture of triumph and smug pleasure. "You know, I got into some problems when I was growing up. Nothing big time, just . . . stuff. So I dropped the old handle and now I'm Ken Fletcher. Took the name off a buddy who got snuffed." He shrugged. "What's the dif? A rose by any name, right?" He grinned. "And this place . . . not bad, huh? Wouldn't the folks do a few flips in the grave if they could see this?" His eyes narrowed. "It's a long story about how I got this place, but it's all working out fine." He took another swig of his beer. "What are you doing here, anyway? Who's the kid?"

She took a deep breath. "I work for the Matthews family. This is Catherine Matthews' daughter. I thought you'd recognize her," she said carefully.

His slightly soft but still handsome face registered surprise. Then he shrugged, his eyes flickering lightly over the blue-eyed child who stared back with equal disinterest. "Small world, huh?" He looked away from the baby. "I never seen her before." A slow, lewd smile touched his somewhat fleshy mouth. "She never brought the kid." Then the smile faded and he shrugged his shoulders. "That was a bummer, man. The accident. There wasn't much left of her." He looked at his beer. "I've been drinking too much since it happened, too, and that's bad."

She stared at him silently, a sick lump in her throat. It was hard to gauge her brother's reaction to the horrible accident that had killed his lover, the mother of the child gazing so innocently up at him. In spite of Eleanor's desire to slip back into her childhood love for Richard, she suspected that his feelings were surface ones, that the accident and Catherine's death were already in the past, well on the way toward being forgotten.

"So they hired you to take care of the kid, huh?" His brow wrinkled. "Oh, yeah, I remember Cathy mentioning a nurse. It gave her more free time."

Then, as his eyes again passed over the baby with mild curiosity, another memory came to Eleanor. She remembered Richard as a boy, his face distorted. A great sense of peace settled over her and she allowed a smile. She wished she could be with Michael that moment, could see his face when she told him. It was like an omen, her sudden memory, and it gave her the confidence to do what she had to do.

"Richard . . . I had no idea this was your business. But I was coming here to see you. To see Ken Fletcher." She touched his hand and took a quick sip of the drink he had brought her.

He glanced at her hand on his wrist and the quick grin returned. He looked at her. "You sure grew up pretty, sis. It's been a long time. You look different, more relaxed. I like your hair like that, long and loose. Last time I saw you you had one of those bun things on your head and you were wearing a starched uniform." He laughed at her look of astonishment. "I was in a car with some other people down in San Bernardino. I saw you on the street, hurrying into one of the buildings. By the time I turned around, you had disappeared."

Her heart softened and she remembered being small and standing behind his big frame when another boy threatened to throw sand in her face. "You came back?"

He shrugged. "Don't get carried away." His laugh was faintly embarrassed. "I was broke and when I saw you I thought you might be good for a little touch, since you were working and all." Then he looked at the saloon and his chest swelled with unashamed pride. "That's all in the past. Now what can I do for you, since you were looking for me?"

Eleanor knew it was as good an opening as any she would ever have. "Richard, I came down here to talk to you about this land thing between you and Lucas Matthews."

His eyes were expressionless. She plunged on. "I've been working for the Matthews family for a while now, and I've learned something about this deal between you. About the grudge war over the land. I don't know what else to call it, and I don't pretend to understand it, either." Suddenly she was confused. She hadn't opted for dealing with her own brother. Yet her first loyalty was to Kierra and Michael, and she knew that Richard's own safety was at stake, as well.

Fletcher attempted to explain. "Old Matthews has wanted this land for a long time so that he can expand his estate. The old coot has some feudal baron idea about restoring the original estate. But the guy I bought this land from wouldn't sell to Matthews. Now I feel the place has more potential to me as a thriving business than it does for the price the ole man will pay for it." He laughed and looked very pleased with his position. "So I'm not an unreasonable man. I told him he could have the land. At my price." He drained the beer. "He's willing to go one hundred grand for the place, lock, stock, and barrel." He looked into the empty bottle regretfully. "Well, I got a lot of barrels in there. So I told him he could have it—for five times that."

Eleanor felt no surprise. The image of her brother as a small boy began to fade. "Isn't that called blackmail or . . . or robbery, or something?"

He grinned again. "Hardly. I have something he wants, and he has something I want. Money. Lots of it." He looked at her speculatively. "What sent you down here, sis?"

She shook her head, catching his meaning. "It was my own idea."

"Well, now there's some big developer interested in the whole hunk of land around here. He wants to make this into some kind of mountain Beverly Hills or something. But he needs both pieces of property to make it worthwhile, Bloodstone and the saloon, too." He looked around. "I've got a big investment here, and I'm interested in seeing some profit off it. The developer is talking in terms of the same cash but a percentage as well." His eyes, hooded now, looked into hers. "It's nothing personal, sis, just money."

She didn't believe him. "Catherine was personal. Catherine was Dr. Matthews' wife."

He began to smile. "Got big eyes for the rich young recluse, Ellie? That it? Want in now that the wife's out of the way?"

She felt her face flame. "Please, Richard. I just want this . . . this war to stop. Before someone gets hurt. I don't like the tension and the things that are

125

going on. It's bad for the baby, and she's had it rough enough already."

He glanced at the infant. "Cathy wasn't much of a mother, huh? I didn't think she'd be. Her mind was on . . . other things."

The blush refused to fade and she felt herself growing angry. "If the land deal is such a good one, why don't you agree to it and be done with it?"

He looked at a bee that was circling the sticky neck of his warming Coke bottle. Gingerly he lifted it and let the brown contents flow into the dust next to the table. He watched the bee go after the stream. "Because I don't trust the old man. Simple, isn't it? How do I know there isn't a separate deal in this for Matthews? He could be buying my land right out from under me, and the rest is all promises. The outfront bread isn't bad, but it isn't what I want. I don't trust the blonde broad. Norma Vanowen, the realtor. I think she's trying to pull something. I figure she's out to make brownie points with your boyfriend, the history buff. Maybe." He shrugged.

"Dr. Matthews is not my boyfriend," she said hotly. "He's my employer."

"Whatever," he said sullenly into the empty bottle. "I'll just tell you one thing, sister of mine. I sign on the dotted line when I see a notarized signature on a bill of sale. Lucas Matthews, it better say, and that fancy educated grandson of his, too. When I see those names there, then we talk to me about doing likewise. Not before. You can tell them . . ." he got slowly to his feet ". . . that's the word from the horse's mouth." He came over and pulled her into his arms for a quick bear hug. "Nothing personal," he said, embracing her. "Actually, I'm glad to see you again. I get into a little nostalgia every now and

126

then. We should get. . . ."

Eleanor heard the sound but it didn't register. All she knew was that it was loud and ringing. Then she was being thrown to the ground, her brother falling heavily over her. While she was still feeling the rush of her breath being knocked from her lungs, he sprang to his feet.

"What in . . . ?" He stood crouched, like a fighter about to spring.

She shook her head and got heavily to her feet, her eyes going immediately to the child. "Kierra!" But the baby was blinking rapidly in the sun. The bullet had awakened her from a sound sleep. "That . . . that was a shot!" she said, realizing suddenly what had happened.

Richard's face was livid with anger as he glanced around at the peaceful terrain. They were alone. He sat down, his hands shakily reaching for a crumpled pack of cigarettes in his shirt pocket. "What's the matter, doesn't your boyfriend know a brotherly hug when he sees one?"

She gasped at him. "Oh, no! That wasn't Michael! It couldn't have been!"

He looked at her coldly. Then he shrugged. "He was taking a chance on getting you or the kid, but that clan would do anything to get what they want." He inhaled deeply, then tossed the match to the ground. "Anything. I used to think Cathy was some bait to sweeten the deal." He smiled nastily. "But it turned out she was working for herself."

Eleanor turned the stroller around. Her entire body was shaking. "I . . . I don't know anything about that." Her eyes began to blur as she fought off hot tears. She swallowed hard and tasted dust. "Richard—Ken—whoever you are. Please. Isn't this proof, whoever it came from? Please get out of this land thing, Richard. Please! Someone will get hurt! Someone else will die!"

He dragged on the cigarette and stared at her distantly, his eyes continually scanning the area for danger. His voice was almost bored. "I had my say, sis. When I see his John Doe on the deal, all legal and tight, then come see me."

She opened her mouth to try once more, but instead she turned and began to walk away. Heart aching, sick with fear and frustration, she knew there was absolutely nothing more to say.

CHAPTER TWELVE

S HE CAME TO THE gray boulders and then exhaustion took over. Finding a relatively clean path of hard earth, Eleanor spread out a blanket and placed the baby on it, making sure that the shade from a large ponderosa pine tree shielded the baby's delicate skin from the rays of the sun. It was a burning ball over the horizon, setting lazily, hotly, baking the abundant vegetation a final hour before sinking behind the mountains for the night.

After surrounding the little one with the yellow duck and the nearly completed panda bear, Eleanor settled wearily at the foot of the rocks to ponder her afternoon and to allow herself to totally surrender to the waves of panic she felt but had managed to repress until returning home. She had almost been killed. She had felt the rush of air as the bullet sped by her. If she had not received the blow, she might have witnessed the death of her brother or even of the baby she loved. She shivered uncontrollably.

In a few moments the panic passed. With the lessening of her emotional reaction she coaxed her mind into functioning again. She had to think before returning to the family. She had to decide who had fired that shot.

Her brother's words returned to her mind, and she forced herself to consider them dispassionately. She rebelled against the thought that Michael might have fired the gun on them. But she couldn't deny to herself that outside of a great deal of feeling between them, she really knew very little about the man she loved. And some of what she did know revealed him to be a man of hidden passion and emotion. She felt sure that he was in love with her. *Could he possibly have followed me to the saloon,* she asked herself achingly, *and could seeing me in Richard's arms, with no idea that he was my brother, have caused something to snap inside Michael? He could have thought it was Catherine all over again.*

Then she remembered the shot. *He would have had to intended to take a gun to Richard all the time. He would have had to bring the gun with him.* She knew he had not loved Catherine in a deep, husbandly way. *But how much could he take of Lucas' taunting, his slurs on Michael's manhood? No!* she thought fiercely, *it couldn't have been Michael!* She couldn't deal with logical concepts. She just knew it hadn't been Michael because her heart told her so. She thought of Kierra. *Michael wouldn't shoot at his own child, no matter what!*

Then logic again interceded and reminded her of the conversation she'd overheard the day of the funeral. She thought of the information which would change his and the old man's feelings about the child. With great sadness she realized that she could not go into the house and tell Michael what she knew. From some deep pool of understanding inside her, she knew he must come to love the child for herself and not for who she was. She felt very old and burdened by the flash of insight.

A part of her mind accepted the possibility that Lucas Matthews could have fired that shot. *He hates Richard. He resents having his grandson lose face in the town he's fought all his life. He would like to kill Richard.* In spite of the hard cold streak—the badge of a man who'd battled his way to the top—she liked the old man. Yet she sensed he was capable of anything in his quest to get his own way. *But to risk shooting the baby or myself?* And yet he had expressed his wishes to erase Kierra from his life. *Seeing Richard and myself together that way . . . He might have thought I was no better than Catherine.*

As she sat by the rock watching the baby, Eleanor realized that the police must have a difficult time with suspects. Once she put her mind to it, she could find reasons for everyone firing that shot. Mrs. Sanchez hated Richard because she feared he might drive Lucas to committing murder. Eleanor remembered the incident of the butterfly, never really far from her mind. *She loves Lucas, but she also has a cold strange place. She asked me to do a terrible thing in the name of love. What would she do for her love?* Only Ricardo and Norma seemed exempt from consideration. She tried especially hard to find motivation for Norma, but ran into endless blind alleys. Norma claimed to want to help the owners of Bloodstone, but Eleanor couldn't conceive of her "help" including murder. Not even for what Richard had called "brownie points." And Ricardo seemed the most normal and uncomplicated of all. *Or is it only that I haven't dug deeply enough? Is everyone hiding under a mask?*

She glanced at her wristwatch. It was time to bathe and feed Kierra. Slowly she put the baby back in the stroller and shook out the blanket. "Well, pumpkin, time for the less exciting part of the day."

* * *

For the first time, the baby was more interested in staying awake and watching her carousel revolve than slipping into sleep. While Kierra's alertness gave Eleanor great pleasure, she couldn't help being impatient. She had to talk to Lucas about her brother. She needed also to see his reaction to her news of the shot. *Perhaps he and Michael wouldn't want me to remain at Bloodstone once I tell them Ken Fletcher's my brother.* She found herself deliberating, finding reasons not to mention any part of her visit to the saloon. But in the end she knew she had to do it.

On her way down the hallway, after Kierra was finally asleep, Eleanor looked hopefully for Michael. Since the funeral she had seen him only infrequently. He was in the process of working out his marriage and death of his wife in his own way. *But not with a gun!* she prayed silently.

The old man answered her knock gruffly.

"Excuse me, Mr. Matthews, but it's important I speak to you if you have a few minutes."

The man turned from his massive wood desk and put down the old-fashioned fountain pen he had been holding. His lined face creased further into a broad surprisingly warm smile. "I can always find time for a pretty girl."

With professional second nature, Eleanor quickly observed Lucas' coloring, the expression on his face, the way he moved. She knew that the old man was secretly in pain a good deal of the time, and while she respected his privacy, she worried about him. *What if he feels he's on borrowed time?* Would it be so difficult to imagine he might feel a desperate need to quickly accomplish his last goal before dying?

"I went to see Ken Fletcher at the saloon a little while ago." She watched the surprise on his face change to a careful wariness. Again he was the hooded eagle, watching, waiting.

"I went because I thought someone not directly involved might be able to reason with him about selling land." She felt a blush begin. "I . . . I know it was none of my business, but I was afraid that something else would happen. I was . . . afraid that Michael might do something drastic." Now that she was putting her feelings into words, she felt hopelessly entangled and terribly naked before the old man's sharp gaze.

His face told her he was well equipped to read between the lines. "I see," he said finally. An oddly boyish smile flickered across his thin lips. It was quickly replaced by his former cool expression. "Go on."

She smoothed her long hair nervously. "I went there from a desire to do something, anything. I'd heard about Norma Vanowen's plan, and I was even willing to . . . to go along with the lie."

His face hardened. "That damned boy! He's too

133

damned soft! Too damn easy for his own good! That's how Catherine got around him."

Her face grew hot again. "I'm not Catherine," she interrupted quietly. She watched him reach for a cigarette and his lighter. "And Michael's a man, not a boy." She noticed the overflowing ashtray and sniffed the smoke in the air. "And you're smoking too much."

He looked at her with undisguised astonishment. Then he broke into loud booming laughter. She waited until he finished his coughing spasm, noticing that he still held onto the pack of cigarettes.

"Go on, girl, tell me about it." He nodded, lit the cigarette, and tossed the pack on his desk. "He is a man," he said musingly. "He fights me tooth and nail." An expression of undeniable pride lit his aged face. "When he wins, then he'll be a man." He blew smoke in her direction. "And you're no Catherine, thank God! Go on, tell me what you've done so I can pick up the pieces."

She didn't take offense to his last words. She knew what kind of a man he was. "I thought that if you got your land you would be satisfied. You would stop destroying the relationship between Kierra and her father." She saw his eyes shift. "I know what you think, but Kierra needs her father," she added, placing special emphasis on the word *father*, "and Michael needs her. Maybe through that relationship he can stop despising himself for taking Catherine because she was beautiful, then dropping her like an old toy when he found there was nothing beyond that beauty. Maybe he'll stop hating himself because he didn't care enough to challenge Ken Fletcher."

Suddenly she felt tired, and wearily she sank

down on an old rocking chair near the desk. "I have no right to speak like this. You have every right to fire me—except that I'm helping the baby. I have no business getting involved as I have. I have no excuse, no justification. Except that I care."

"What did Fletcher say?" He tapped ashes off his cigarette into a marble ashtray and looked thoughtful.

She sighed. "I got something of a shock down there. Two shocks, as a matter of fact. Ken Fletcher is an alias. His real name is Richard Lawrence." She took a deep breath. "He's my brother."

"Your brother?" His eyes widened and he leaned forward in his chair.

"Yes. I didn't even know he was anywhere in the area. I haven't seen him for a long time. He got into trouble when he was growing up, and we went our separate ways."

He nodded and sat back, a thoughtful expression on his face.

Eleanor saw that Lucas was willing to believe her as best his suspicious nature would allow. "We talked. I told him that I thought there was too much bad feeling between Bloodstone and the saloon, especially since Catherine's death. I asked him to agree to the land deal and to stop this ugly war before someone else got hurt. I . . .he said. . . .The point is, he's suspicious. He thinks its all a trick to get him to sell his land. He's prepared to sell, but only if you've signed away Bloodstone with an ironclad agreement. Notarized and all."

The old man digested her words, then sighed. "You didn't tell him anything?"

She shook her head. "Nothing. Just that I felt that something bad would happen if this wasn't resolved in a logical manner."

"And the second shock? You said you got two shocks." He pressed what was left of his cigarette against the side of the marble ashtray.

She told him about the shooting, her eyes watching him closely. He listened attentively, asking rapid-fire questions about the direction of the shot, the events which had preceded it and whether, in her opinion, the bullet had been meant as a threat or had actually intended to find a victim.

By the time he was finished Eleanor found herself unsure of just how innocent the old man's reaction to the news had been. He gave her a short lecture of the dangers in getting involved in affairs that weren't her business, and then, in a more kindly voice, thanked her for her concern.

"I was thinking. . . ." She hesitated.

"Yes? Yes? Out with it, girl. You've nothing to fear from me."

She certainly hoped that was the case. "I was thinking that I would talk to Richard—Ken—again, and see if I couldn't convince him to simply sell the land directly to you at a fair sum. Your offer and the contractor's offer aren't really so far apart, especially if there's no chance for later benefits to my brother. If you could meet his offer as far as the actual cash. . . ."

"Oh, are we disturbing anyone?"

Eleanor looked up and saw Norma Vanowen prettily framed in the doorway. Behind her was Michael.

Lucas turned and squinted his eyes. "Nonsense! Haven't let anyone disturb me in fifty years." He gestured them into the room with an impatient motion of his nicotine-stained hand.

Michael's expression revealed curiosity at seeing Eleanor in his grandfather's room, but there was something else in his eyes, a shadowed, harried look that disturbed her. He seemed thinner and paler. Involuntarily Eleanor found herself remembering the shot which had come from nowhere and nearly put an end to her own life. "Hello, Eleanor," he said softly, looking at her.

Norma remembered her manners. "Eleanor! I hardly recognized you without the baby. Where is she, asleep, I'll bet? Sweet little thing, isn't she?" She beamed vaguely in the direction of the young nurse, then turned her full attention to the old man. "Have you a moment, Lucas? It's rather important." She glanced significantly at Eleanor. The young woman got up to leave.

Lucas waved her back into her seat. "This is important, too." Briefly the man related the events of the morning to his grandson and the realtor. At the mention of the family relationship between herself and Ken Fletcher, Eleanor felt Michael's eyes burning into her. She ran her slim fingers over the polished wood on the arms of her chair, then pressed her spine straighter against the crushed velvet of the seat's fabric. She didn't want to examine the expression on his face, didn't want to recall Richard's words about her "boyfriend" not recognizing a brotherly hug. She stared into the faded pattern of lattice work and silver rosebud wallpaper until her eyes smarted and began to tear.

"I see," said Norma thoughtfully when Lucas stopped talking.

Eleanor was relieved that the old man had not thought it necessary to include the part about the gun shot. She imagined he had his own reasons for omitting it. *Perhaps he knew who had fired that shot.*

The blonde woman began to pace the floor. After a moment she stopped in front of Lucas. "Well then, I can only suggest one obvious move. It's our only. . . ." She glanced at Eleanor, still in her chair. "I trust we have your confidence?" she turned to Lucas.

Eleanor knew the realtor didn't want to reveal anything of importance in front of her. She also saw that Norma hoped Lucas would ask her to leave. She sat tight and looked innocently at the blonde.

"What move, girl?" the old man asked with a show of irritation.

"Sign the paper first, of course. Go through with it and then my contractor will sign it back to you. Fletcher will see your names and he'll sign, too. Then we allow a decent interval to pass—during which time the saloon will be long closed—and you'll be able to bring in the wreckers and have what you want, just as you've dreamed. I don't even think there'll be hard feelings." Norma sat down in a straight-backed chair with a look of satisfaction. "Business deals fall through often enough."

"I don't like it. Something could go wrong. Once I put my name on that paper Bloodstone is out of my hands. I don't like it," he repeated, but his voice had a ring of indecision to it.

"But you mustn't!"

Three heads turned toward the nurse. She flushed hotly. "Excuse me. I . . . I know it's not my business. . . ." She glanced at Lucas. "From what my brother said I believe that all he wants is to get out with enough of a stake to satisfy his greed. But I could never be sure that Richard means what he says." She shrugged her shoulders in a gesture of confusion. "I don't know anything about real estate or big business, but it doesn't sound wise to me to risk what you already have to get something you want but don't absolutely need. Once you sign away Bloodstone something might happen."

Two livid red spots appeared on Norma's pale cheeks. "I don't think you understand, dear," she said coolly. "There is no risk here. The contractor is a personal friend and he's consented to operate in name only as a special favor to me. The idea came into being because Paul—the contractor—did entertain the notion of buying up here and creating an exclusive mountain community. But once he understood that Mr. Matthews would never part with his land at any price, he abandoned his plans." She turned back to Lucas. "It is obvious to me that the only way you can get the land is by playing this silly game and signing first. You do trust me, don't you? I can take care of the whole thing."

"I don't think the question of trust was raised, Norma. But as a seasoned businessman I realize Eleanor here is making a valid point. If I dropped dead we'd be in a fine mess, wouldn't we?"

"Nonsense," the realtor said smoothly, "you'll outlive us all."

"I . . . I think I'd better check the baby," Eleanor said, rising.

"Wait . . . let me." Michael left the room.

Eleanor wondered if he had wanted to see Kierra or if he had simply wanted out of the room. Immediately she felt ashamed of the thought.

"We'll have to think of something else, Norma. Fletcher signs or we forget the whole business." The old man reached out for his cigarettes and mumbled a soft curse when he pulled out one that had broken in half. He tossed it into the wastepaper basket by his desk, then took another cigarette from the pack. He looked at it suspiciously, then put it in his mouth.

"I fail," the realtor said as Eleanor got up, "to understand why, after all this time you would choose to listen to this . . . this nursemaid and not to me."

"I'd better go check the baby," Eleanor said hastily, moving to the door. "Excuse me, please."

As she left Norma's strained voice followed her.

"I've tried to be helpful."

"Now, this is nothing personal against you, Norma," Lucas reassured her. . . .

Eleanor hurried so she would have to hear as little as possible. She felt uncomfortable in having taken the blonde woman on as an enemy. Somehow she knew that behind the smiling pretty face was a dangerous, treacherous person, prepared to do whatever necessary to get her own way.

Michael Matthews stood over the crib, the infant cradled in his arms. The fingers of one hand were softly touching the blonde curls, and on his face was an expression of pained pleasure.

"Oh, she's up," Eleanor said when she could speak. She looked at them through a film of sudden tears. It was so good, seeing the baby in her father's arms.

Kierra blinked sleepy eyes at Eleanor, then looked up at Michael. Her little head swung back to her nurse and, for the very first time her mouth curved into a full, radiant smile.

Eleanor felt the tears slipping down her cheeks and then she was laughing and reaching out to hug the man and the baby. Arms were around her, and the scent of powder and baby oil filled her nostrils as she touched soft arms that were just beginning to reach back.

"She knows you, she really does." Michael's laugh was warm and happy-sounding. His arms held her tightly. "Oh, Eleanor."

The baby was now equally in her arms as their lips met. For a second Eleanor lost track of where she was. Then the baby squealed from the sudden pressure of their bodies moving together, and Michael released his hold. "I . . .I'd better get back before Norma and my grandfather come to blows." He gave Eleanor the baby and dropped a soft kiss on her head. "I'll see you later, okay?"

She nodded, too overwhelmed to speak. Hugging the baby to her breast, she watched Michael leave the room. "Feel my heart, darling? I think it's going to explode."

Her happy bubble lasted throughout the baby's feeding and changing, and when she carried Kierra down the stairs to her stroller she listened carefully to find out if Lucas still had company. She heard nothing. Although it was threatening to darken outside, she felt an urge to take a short walk before dinner. She considered bringing Kierra to the dinner table for meals and getting the men back on a normal schedule. Kierra was a part of the family, and the sooner her presence was accepted by Lucas Matthews, the sooner life at Bloodstone would take on a semblance of congeniality. She thought of telling the old man what she had found out earlier that day, but again felt deeply that it was important for Kierra's father and great-grandfather to come to love her for herself.

The house was very silent and looked as if it had

just been given a rub with a polished cloth. Eleanor had always liked this time of day, when the fading rays of the sun cast its last caressing eye, softening and shining all it touched. From the kitchen came the definite odor of a well-seasoned roast, along with the crisp fragrance of vegetables and the penetrating, lingering scent of freshly picked herbs and spices.

She let herself and the baby out through a side door. Only the boulders behind the house rejected the warmth of the declining sunlight, huge and gray and once again menacing in contrast to the vivid greens and browns and rusts of the summery forest. She looked away from them and pushed the stroller out into the wilderness, past tall trees which canopied them as they walked.

The air was slightly moist, filled with promise of still another summer storm. Eleanor heard dried leaves crumbling under her step, relinquishing their own special crushed fragrance to her. *It's a magic day,* she thought, again forgetting the bullet which might have killed her. She could think only of Michael's lips on hers, his nearness, the promise of a future in which neither would ever have to be lonely again. . . .

She wandered deeper into the trees, watching the setting sun alter the colors from moment to moment. Small chipmunks scampered nearby, bustling around like children playing one last game before being called home to dinner. The happiness she felt transformed the forest into a fairyland, and even the baby seemed enraptured by the sounds and smells and sights. A squirrel raced by with something in its mouth, and just as it was about to scurry up a tree it stopped dead, its little head cocked to one side. Eleanor heard a low growl and turned also.

In a clearing between two maple trees stood a very large dog. Eleanor recognized it as a sleek Doberman pinscher. Instinctively she stepped a little closer to the baby in her stroller. She had never seen the animal before, but something about him told her that he was capable of killing both of them. The growl grew louder and the two burning eyes were focused with fierce intensity on her. Keeping her eyes on him, Eleanor slowly pushed the stroller toward a thicket of trees.

She had never been afraid of dogs. If Kierra hadn't been with her she might have cautiously approached the Doberman, hands outstretched to show she meant no harm. But with the tiny child she didn't dare. Her only thought was to push the stroller to the relative safety of the trees. Then she would try to distract the animal. If the creature were rabid she would somehow manage to lead it away from the baby.

The dog stood as still as a statue with only his muscled chest in motion, heaving excitedly. Eleanor watched the rapid breathing, wondering if the dog was sick or just tense with anticipation. He didn't advance as she slowly moved. Cautiously she reached the safety of the trees. She parked the stroller and began to edge away from it, back into the darkening clearing. The hot eyes were still on her, and the growling began as soon as she moved.

Eleanor looked around for the dog's owner, but she didn't dare call out. She stood still until the dog stopped growling, and then took another few steps away from where the stroller was sitting. She stopped when the Doberman suddenly began to move toward her, taking another step only when he was again still. She continued this maneuver until, with no warning, the dog sprang.

Panic overtook her senses when the big black dog moved on her. She screamed, then started to run. All she could think of was Kierra, alone and defenseless, easy prey to the dog. She ran for the nearest tree just as she felt the weight of the dog thrusting itself against the back of her thighs. She screamed again then fell, twisting as she hit the ground. The tree flew up at her as she dropped and tumbled her easily into unconsciousness.

The last thing she felt was pain in the back of her head. And—distantly—she heard a shrill whistle cut through the louder sounds of the animal bending over her. . . .

CHAPTER THIRTEEN

S HE AWOKE TO A strange sound, something
between the bleating of a sheep and the whimpering
of a puppy. She lay very still, listening, wondering.
It occurred to her that she rested on a bed of earth,
pine needles, and leaves. Small pebbles and twigs
were part of her mat as well and she began to feel
pain all over her body. It wasn't until she sat up that
the stunning ache in the back of her head took precedence over the other minor hurts. Slowly, winc-
ingly, she got to her feet, steadied herself against
the tree, listened again to the strange sounds from
nearby and remembered.

"Oh, God!" She peered into the darkness,
thankful that the baby was crying, unsure she could
find the stroller in the darkness without some kind
of guide. "Kierra! Here I am! I'm coming!"

She hurried in spite of her headache. "Baby," she
whispered, reaching into the stroller and picking up

the infant. "You must be starved! I don't even know how late it is!" She held the child close and looked up toward the sky. The dark leaves of the trees hid all but a few stars, enough to tell the nurse that she had lain unconscious in the forest for several hours. She remembered the horrible dog, could still feel it throwing her to the ground. She took a moment to marvel that she was alive at all. Then she recalled the high-pitced whistle she seemed to have heard just as she became unconscious, and she wondered who had called the dog off. Even more significant was the question of who had set the animal against her in the first place?

As she put the baby back down in the stroller, once she'd stopped crying, Eleanor realized that for the first time Kierra had cried out when things were not going her way. She had felt loneliness and hunger and the wetness of her diaper, and she had sent out a protest against such treatment. Professionally Eleanor knew this marked a very important milestone in the baby's progress. While she was sorry Kierra had had to suffer, she was well pleased with the results. "We'll get you home in a minute, darling. Then dry and fed. How does that sound?" She brushed dirt and dry leaves from her Levi's and sweater. The headache was fading rapidly. By the time the house loomed as a bright beacon before them the nurse felt almost normal again.

She entered through a side door closest to the stairwell where she kept the stroller. The house was warm and smelled delicious, and Eleanor realized she, too, was famished. She parked the stroller, then picked up the baby and went upstairs to the nursery without seeing anyone, though she thought she heard Lucas' voice.

Her dinner was waiting on a tray on her dresser, cooling. She gave it a hungry glance, then got busy changing and feeding the baby. Kierra was half asleep by the time the last spoonful of pureed peaches was between her little lips. Eleanor quickly washed her face and tucked her into the crib. "Good night, darling," she said, kissing the sweet cheeks which were now rosy. "Sleep tight." She tucked the comforter around the child, then shut off the light.

She refused to think as she quickly washed and began to eat her cold dinner. There was too much to think about, and most of it frightened her. Yet thoughts creeped in despite her intentions, and her appetite diminished. *That dog was after me,* she admitted, putting down her fork. *He was sent to find and attack me!* She recalled in absolute detail the stance of the Doberman, the way his intense eyes had followed her, the way he had come after her. . . . *He might have killed me . . . someone sent him to kill me. . . .* Then she remembered the shrill whistle. *Whoever it was changed his mind. Or was it deliberate? Maybe they didn't intend to kill me at all . . . maybe they wanted to frighten me, give me some kind of a warning. . . .* Her mind felt hot, fevered. *Who would want to hurt me? Who would want to frighten me?*

A knock at the door disturbed her thoughts. She answered it quickly, hoping that Michael would be there. She needed to see him, talk to him.

Ricardo flashed his easy grin. "I have come for the tray, if you have finished, Miss Lawrence. Also to tell you that Dr. Matthews sends his apologies but will not be able to see you until tomorrow. He is detained with his grandfather."

Eleanor noted the slight elevation of the young

147

man's eyebrows and knew that Michael and Lucas had once again locked horns. She hid her disappointment as best she could. "Thank you." She brought him the tray.

He started to leave, then turned back to her. "It is a lonely life you have chosen to live here," he said carefully. "Tell me, why is it you stay?" But instead of waiting for an answer, the young Mexican turned and left the room, the tray casually balanced on one palm. The door shut softly behind him.

She stared at the closed door, then returned to her chair. It seemed as if the question had not come from Ricardo as much as through him, as if the question had hung waiting in the air from the moment she had arrived. *Why have I stayed here?* she asked herself. Her first thought was of the baby, and her second of Michael. *Two excellent reasons,* she assured herself. But then she thought of the bullet she had narrowly avoided, and of the big dog. She glanced in at the nursery. Kierra was better every day, no longer in real danger. Any nurse who was conscientious and able could take care of her now. *She didn't really need me now!*

Then she thought of how close she had taken the little baby to injury or possible death that very day. It was possible that she had been the target for that bullet and not Richard, and whoever wanted her dead or away proved himself unmindful of the safety of a small child. *Maybe my being here is putting Kierra's life in danger!* she thought, growing increasingly agitated. *But who would want me out of the way?* It was an absurd question, yet the evidence spoke for itself. Either it was all a ghastly coincidence and the bullet was meant for Richard, as she first thought, or it was indeed meant for her. *Either*

*the dog was just an ill-tempered pet who had
wandered into the wilderness and taken an instant
dislike to me, or someone sent that animal in there
for one reason only. . . .*

She felt sticky and dirty, and her bruises began to
hurt again. Without thinking, she propelled her
body through the ritual of undressing, showering,
brushing her teeth, and getting into a nightgown
and robe. Mercifully, she was exhausted. It would
be heaven to slip into sleep and not have to think.
She slid between the cool sheets and turned her hot
cheek to the crisp, sweet-smelling pillow slip. *To
sleep and not think. . . .*

Yet tired as she was, the thoughts came unbid-
den, seeping into her tired brain, recreating scenes,
suggesting nightmares, teasing her until exhaustion slipped away and left her mind alive and
thirsting for knowledge at any cost. *No*, she
thought, *the dog had to be an accident! And the
bullet—perhaps we're both wrong. Couldn't it have
been a hunter, a green, inept hunter who had
wandered too close to the main road and shot wild?*
She occupied herself with pleasant deceptions for a
few desperate moments, then regained enough control to face what had happened straight on. She
didn't need anyone to tell her that the incident with
the dog had been deliberate—she had known it the
moment she had laid eyes on the creature in the
clearing. Now it was up to her to determine who it
was that would do such a thing. From there the only
way to go was to make some very important deci-
sions. Foremost was to decide if her staying at
Bloodstone posed a real threat to Kierra's safety. If
so, she had to leave, no matter what her feelings.
But first she had to know who was trying to hurt

her, perhaps trying to kill her.

The crushed butterfly came to her mind, and, with the image, a long view of the Mexican housekeeper. Eleanor felt she had mental access to both sides of the woman—the place she held hatred and the place love dwelled. She could not believe the housekeeper would try to kill her, but she couldn't dismiss the possibility that she might go to lengths to scare her away. *Without me here Kierra might be shunted off to relatives. She believes that Kierra is the breaking point in Lucas' patience. She might do anything to keep Lucas calm!* A memory of the night she and Jim had first come to Bloodstone to treat the old man for stroke came to her mind. *Teresa Sanchez would remember that night even more vividly and she would go to any length to avoid a repetition. . . .*

Uneasily dismissing Teresa for the moment, Eleanor thought of the housekeeper's son. But she could find no motive or clue, and rapidly moved on to Norma Vanowen. She had no idea of the realtor's inner self, but she felt an instinctive distrust for the woman. Somehow she knew that behind the constant smile was deception and malice, but again she could find no motive or indication that anything was amiss. Reluctantly she thought about Lucas. She had no idea of the ownership of the dog, but in spite of her genuine liking for the old man she put nothing past him. *He certainly could have fired that gun,* she thought. *But so could have Michael!* As soon as the thought formed itself Eleanor hated herself for it. *Michael wouldn't hurt me! He wouldn't hurt his own child!*

Then she remembered that he didn't know Kierra was his. She thought hard about her decision not to tell him the facts at once. *If he knew that Richard was sterile as a result of the mumps we had both contracted years ago, he would accept her!* But something stubborn inside her wanted better than that for the child she loved with her whole heart. She wanted Kierra's place in the family to come from the child alone. *Maybe I'm fooling myself. Maybe I'm risking the baby for some ideal that makes no more sense than anything else that goes on in this house! Maybe at base all men are this way, loving what was there for the sake of ego and masculinity. Maybe. . . .*

With an effort she forced herself to abandon the line of thinking. She needed to consider the facts as she knew them. If she believed that Michael, for reasons she couldn't understand, was responsible for the near accidents, she had no choice but to leave. If it was Michael, she would have to initiate Kierra's move to some other family. *Perhaps they weren't perfect, but it would be better than abandoning her to a deranged father.* But an image of Michael's compassionate face shattered the painful picture of ultimate deceit and treachery.

She turned her thoughts back to Lucas. *I have no choice but to believe that it's the old man and that he wants me out, but for some reason doesn't dare request that I leave.*

Yet something was still wrong with her thinking. Nothing felt as if it fit, as if it made the kind of sense she was looking for. *There's something more here, something I don't see. . . .* With that thought she fell asleep.

CHAPTER FOURTEEN

A VIOLENT ARGUMENT raged in her brain. It transformed itself into an angry sea which rose and fell in crashing waves, splattering the walls of her bedroom with foam. That foam reminded her of the Doberman. She saw eyes that glittered and a mouth that foamed and said terrible things in a muted, furious voice. The sea crashed again, upsetting her, shaking her body as she slept. Then she was in bed in the ornate hallway, with only the light from the fish tanks to tell her that Michael was fighting with the dog . . . no, it was Michael and Lucas . . . Michael and Lucas. . . .

From a long ways off a door slammed and footsteps walked off into eternity. The silence rang out, tensing her ears and increasing the restlessness she felt. She tried to curl up inside herself, to settle back into dreamless sleep, to merge with the total silence until she and it were the same. . . .

Eleanor opened her eyes slowly, blinking in the darkness, her head raising from the pillow to listen for sounds that weren't there. As soon as she awakened she knew that she had been only half asleep, that the terrible argument she had dreamed had really taken place in the hallway moments before. A glance at her clock told her that it was nearly morning. She sat up and wondered if Michael and his grandfather had been up fighting all night long. Since they had carried their argument into the hall, she thought it likely that one of the men had been on his way somewhere outside the house. Immediately she envisioned Michael striking off for the saloon again, and she was afraid. She felt terrible anger toward the old man, wondering how far Lucas had provoked him. She couldn't help thinking of the bullet that had missed her so narrowly the day before.

Eleanor dressed quickly. She had little more than an hour and a half before Kierra would awaken. Impatiently she dragged her brush through her long dark hair, then grabbed a sweater from the drawer. She closed the door quietly and prayed that Kierra wouldn't wake up early. Fortunately, the baby stayed on a consistent schedule but still she planned to tell Ricardo of her absence.

The hallway was dim and silent. The doors to all the rooms were neatly shut and the fish tanks glowed with their eternal luminescence. She glanced at Michael's door, then hurried down the stairs hoping that someone would be up.

She found Mrs. Sanchez in the kitchen. The two women exchanged quick glances. The older one nodded. "He has gone." She looked old and helpless.

"Where?" Eleanor half turned toward the closest

exit, the many-paned door leading from the kitchen to the little garden and beyond, to the boulders and the pathway she had taken many times before.

The Mexican woman shrugged, her ample shoulders barely moving. "I did not hear so much. Only the anger, the hatred. I think he has gone to see the young saloon man. He has never left like this." Her eyes were reproachful. "If the child were no longer here. . . ."

Eleanor shook her head impatiently. "Well, she's here. And she's staying here. Where she belongs!" She turned her back on the other and made a special effort to remain calm. "I can't talk. I have to find Michael before . . . before something happens."

"Michael?"

Eleanor stopped at the surprise in the woman's voice. "Yes. Of course. I'm afraid. . . ."

"But Mr. Michael is in his room. He did not leave the house. Only his grandfather is gone." Her face softened and her naturally melodic voice trembled. "It is the grandfather. Lucas. You will go after him?" She looked down. "Lucas?" The name was a caress on her lips. "I cannot go. It is not my place."

The nurse sat down on a small stepladder that was open next to the wall. "Lucas," she said softly, relief flooding through her. Then she looked up and gave in to a wave of compassion. "Yes, of course I will go. Did he take the car?"

"*Sí*. He cannot walk very far." The housekeeper turned her dark eyes to the floor. "I hope that is all he took." She looked at her hands. "I pray he did not take his gun."

"His gun? Do you think. . . ?"

"I do not know. I do not know!"

Eleanor felt her heart begin to pound. "Is Ricardo

154

with him? Or did he drive himself?"

"Ricardo is outside, in the garden. *Señor* Matthews took the car himself." She touched her weathered fingers to the loose gray-streaked hair coiled on her head.

Eleanor nodded and went outside. At first she didn't see anyone, then she noticed that the door to the small shed was open. "Ricardo?"

He came to the doorway. "Good morning, Miss Lawrence. You are up very early, I see." His grin was wry. "But you are not the only one."

She touched his arm urgently. "Ricardo, please, I'm going after Mr. Matthews. I should be back soon but would you watch Kierra for me? In case she gets up. If you could just look in on her every so often if I'm not back. Please don't let her cry."

He stared at her. "Why are you going after him?"

She didn't know how to answer. His soft voice and black eyes held her. "This craziness is not your business, pretty nurse." He paused. "Let them kill each other." His voice dropped to a whisper. "It will come to that in time, anyway. Why do you risk your own life? You cannot stop what must happen at this house. Others have died here, and more will yet die!"

She stared back at him, mute in the knowledge that he was telling her what he believed firmly to be the truth. "You're right," she admitted. "It's not my business. But I know something about the child, and I must tell Mr. Matthews before it's too late."

He looked at her searchingly then nodded. "You have some knowledge that the child is a Matthews, *si?* And you believe that bringing this knowledge to the old man will put an end to the bad feeling between the saloon owner and this house?"

"Yes! Of course!" The air was crisp. She felt chilled.

He shook his head sadly. "You are mistaken, pretty nurse. Your news will change nothing! It is not the child over which they fight." His dark eyes clouded. "Don't you know that? Can't you sense it? There is something else that bothers the old man. Something old, as old as him. Something ugly. It eats at him like a cancer. It will not let him die in peace. It was here long before the child and will go on until the land is his or he is dead."

"Do . . . do you know what it is?" she whispered, not wishing to believe him but powerless to resist the conviction in his voice.

The young Mexican shook his head again. "No." He looked up and watched the great ball of the sun begin its slow journey across the sky. "I do not know, but somehow I have the feeling that soon we shall all know." He looked at her again, and the hint of a patient ageless smile touched his lips. "And perhaps then," he said very softly, "we shall wish for our lost ignorance."

She looked away from him. "Still I must. go. Please watch the baby. It's getting late and I. . . ."

A scream sliced through the morning air. Eleanor turned to the house but Ricardo was already tugging at the kitchen door. She entered right behind his lean back.

"Mama! What is it?"

Teresa Sanchez stared at them, the telephone still in her hand. She closed her expressive eyes and remained silent a moment longer, as if exhausted by her scream. Her dark complexion had paled.

"Mama?"

She opened her eyes and looked at Eleanor. "It is

the *señor*. He has shot the saloon man, Fletcher. It is his lawyer on the telephone. Please, miss, ask Mister Michael to take the call."

Ricardo put a steadying hand on his mother's arm, then started for the door. "I'll call him. Sit down, Mama."

The older woman shook her head. "No. I am all right. It was just the . . . the shock." She turned to Eleanor. "I feared this. I knew something would happen." Her voice sounded drained but it was free of accusation. "The child, she was the final insult. He could not take the betrayal."

"Mrs. Sanchez," Eleanor said, "the child is Michael's." She turned the heavier woman so that she could see the truth in her eyes. "Ken Fletcher—is he. . . ?" She couldn't bring herself to release the word.

The woman shook her head quickly. "No. He is in the hospital, but he will live." She touched her flushed cheek. "It is true? The child is of this family?"

"Yes. Ken Fletcher is my brother. When we were children we had a disease called mumps. As a result, Richard—Ken—is sterile. The child couldn't be his. Kierra is Michael's daughter." She wished fervently she had shared this information the day before with Lucas Matthews. *Maybe this wouldn't have happened.* Then she recalled Ricardo's words, and intuitively she knew the young man had spoken the truth. Whatever had led to this shooting was a long time in the coming, had begun long before there was a Kierra.

"I should have known. . . . Forgive me. . . ."

Eleanor nodded absently, thinking now of Lucas rather than the child. In the background she could hear the rapid beat of two sets of legs hurrying down the stairs followed by Michael's breathless "Hello?" from the phone in the library. The rest was muffled. "What will they do to Lucas?" She cringed at the thought of the old man in some bleak jail, whatever he had done. "Did they arrest him?"

A look of pain crossed the housekeeper's face. "*Sí.* They arrested him, but he's sick. He, too, is in the hospital. He has had another stroke!" She sealed in the agony by closing her eyes. "The lawyer said he is not having pain. He said . . . he will soon be well. . . ." Her voice broke and she began to sob quietly into her hands.

"He'll be all right," Eleanor soothed, putting an arm around the older women. When Teresa Sanchez was in control of herself again, the nurse left her side and picked up the phone. She called Jim at home, hung up, then tried the hospital. "Dr. Munroe, please."

Jim came to the phone just as Michael and Ricardo entered the kitchen. Little Kierra, eyes blinking sleepily, was in Ricardo's arms. At the sight of her nurse, the little girl began to whimper. "Jim? Eleanor. Just a second, please." She covered the mouthpiece and whispered to Ricardo. "Her bottle's already warming next to the crib. Please give it to her and, oh, do you know how to change a diaper?"

The dark young man smiled gravely. "I have the feeling that I shall now learn." He patted his mother's hand as he left the room.

Eleanor turned her attention to the voice on the phone. In the space of a few seconds she had learned that Lucas had had a very minor stroke and that the bullet, which had punctured Ken's spleen, had been removed and that his condition was satisfactory.

Then she hung up and gave Michael a quick hug.

He relaxed slightly and patted Mrs. Sanchez' shoulder. "Is there coffee?"

After they were settled at the huge kitchen table, coffee cups warming their hands, Michael related the lawyer's words. "Someone heard the shot, apparently, and called the sheriff. When Bill and his partner arrived at the saloon they found Fletcher on the floor with the bullet wound and my grandfather was standing over him. They had no choice but to arrest him. They didn't find the gun, but they're combing the woods for it now. Grandfather had his stroke before the ambulance got there, so he apparently hasn't had a chance to say much." He looked down at his coffee.

At that moment Norma burst into the kitchen, her blonde hair immaculately coiffed in a tight French roll. She looked beautiful in beige slacks and a matching blouse, but her perfect face was agitated. "No one answered my knock. Oh, Michael, I just heard! I've come to drive you to the hospital. I can't tell you how terrible I feel."

He got up. "Yes. Of course." He glanced absently at his slightly wrinkled blue suit. "I'm ready." He looked questioningly at Eleanor.

She rose. "I'm going, too. I must talk to Lucas."

Norma stared at her, the concern replaced by a look of incredulity. "You? Whatever for? I'm sure there are more than enough nurses."

Michael put an arm around the dark-haired girl's waist. "If she wants to go, Norma. . . ."

Eleanor nodded. "I have to talk to him. I have something he must hear."

Again the expression on the realtor's face shifted. This time Eleanor read pure and complete hatred.

"I doubt very much if Lucas needs to hear anything from a . . . a servant at the moment."

Michael turned sharply to the blonde woman. "Norma! Eleanor has never been a servant in this house." He looked at the nurse and again put his arm around her. "Eleanor is going to be my wife when all this is over." He smiled down at her. "Or am I being presumptuous?"

She couldn't speak. Instead she leaned against his arm and let her feelings show in the sudden rush of color in her cheeks and the shine in her eyes.

"Shall we go?" he asked, giving the nurse a squeeze and turning toward the blonde woman.

"Do you want to come?" Eleanor stopped by Teresa Sanchez' chair.

The housekeeper smiled faintly. "No, miss. I will wait here, where I belong, where I always wait."

* * *

The drive seemed endless as Norma navigated the turns and twists with cold competence. Eleanor felt the tension in the other woman, but when they pulled into the last turn before reaching the flatlands, Norma turned to her with some trace of her usual bright self.

"This has been a strain on all of us, Eleanor. Please forgive me if I was rude before. I was upset and I wasn't thinking. I also want to congratulate both of you. I'm sure you'll be very happy." She flashed a sudden disarmingly girlish smile. "You wouldn't hold a few sour grapes against a girl, would you?" Her long-lashed eyes flickered over Michael's handsome face with open affection.

Michael smiled distractedly, then went back to

his silent thinking. Eleanor made herself smile back, but inside she felt the same weight of suspicion and dislike. Something told her that Norma was conning her. The prettily phrased apology sounded right, even modest, but it lacked the ring of sincerity. *Something's wrong. She wants me to feel as if I've pulled something over her. Why? What does she want?*

Michael met the lawyer in the hospital lobby. He nodded pleasantly to both women. "They only allow one visitor at a time here. Perhaps you might take turns visiting Mr. Matthews while I brief Michael?"

Taking the hint, the two women rode the elevator to the fifth floor. Eleanor waited in the visitor's room while Norma went in to see Lucas. While she waited her turn, Eleanor stared at the aquamarine walls and tried to keep her mind a blank. She'd find the words she needed once she was with the old man.

Norma returned shortly. "I think he's going to be just fine." She sat down on the blue lounge and lit a cigarette. "I suppose he's really going to be in trouble now." She sighed sympathetically.

Eleanor got up hastily. "I'd better go."

"Oh, I just ran into your doctor friend. He's very attractive, isn't he?" Her smile revealed perfect teeth.

Eleanor looked at the teeth. *Like a barracuda*, she thought. "Yes. Is he with Mr. Matthews?"

"Yes." She tapped ashes into a stainless steel ashtray. "Very attractive."

Eleanor left the room quickly, hoping she would have time enough alone with the old man.

"Ellie!"

She turned and then Jim's arms were around her.

She stepped back. "How are you?"

His blue eyes were red-rimmed. "Well, it's been a long night. He smiled. "Better, now that I see you." He looked at her. "That's no place for you to be, Ellie. Come back to work for me. If you don't want the other. . . ." He shrugged. "I won't press. But at least come back to work."

Looking up into his face, Eleanor found the offer intensely desirable. She loved Michael, but slipping out from under the entanglements at Bloodstone sounded inviting. *I could go back to work for Jim and only have a love affair that goes nowhere to worry about.* "We'll see, Jim. Let me think about it, will you? Now I have to see Mr. Matthews."

"Promise you'll consider it?"

"I promise." But even as she spoke, Eleanor knew that she had no decision to make. *It had already been made—the day I came to that house. The day I saw Kierra. The day I met Michael.* She thought of Michael's promise of marriage, and instead of the great welling joy his words had first prompted, she felt a terrible depression. She knew that there was so much yet that had to come before they could be together. *So many questions to be answered. So much I don't understand! If Lucas has done this to Richard, what is it he hopes to gain? Now Richard will never sell. And if the objective was honor for the family because of Catherine, what honor is there to die in a jail cell?*

The old man seemed surprised and pleased to see the young nurse, though he spent the first few minutes complaining of the poor care he was receiving.

She interrupted his diatribe. "Mr. Matthews, there's something I must tell you." She told him about her brother's sterility in full detail. "So there was no reason for shooting Richard. And now you're in trouble. I should have told you yesterday." She laughed sadly, apologetically. "I've read fairy tales all of my life. I wanted a happy ending without making it happen."

He nodded, a far-away look in his eyes. His graying head sank back into the pillows. Then he reached out and touched the nurse's long hair gently. His dry voice sounded tired. "I'm glad about the girl. But I didn't shoot Fletcher."

She looked up in surprise.

"I found him on the ground when I arrived. He told me that unless I signed the land agreement he would swear that I had shot him. I told him I'd rot in jail first!" The last was delivered with some of his old fire.

"But you can't, if you didn't shoot him!" Eleanor took his ancient hand. "You don't deserve it. No one will believe him."

His eyes softened. "Won't they? Everyone knows Lucas Matthews would kill a man who refused him his land and took his grandson's wife. But what does it matter? The wheel of life spins in a perfect circle, girl. My mother was an Indian, and she told me that many times." The far-away look returned to his misted eyes. "It's my turn to pay, Ellie. My time in the desert." He looked at her. "My only regret is that Bloodstone will never again be as it once was. The way I wanted to leave it for Michael."

The question had been waiting to be asked for so long. "Why is that so important? There's more than enough land as it is. Why do you need Bloodstone to be its original size?" She stroked his trembling hand.

He looked at the visitor's chair by the bed. "Sit down, child, and I'll tell you a story." He waited until she was seated and her hand was back in his. "It should have been told long ago. I was fool enough to believe I could die without telling it. I grew up in Los Angeles with my mother. We starved some of the time and ate garbage the rest. It wasn't until I was eighteen that I found out Bloodstone should have been mine."

"I don't understand."

He smiled sadly. "My mother kept house for St. Clair, who built the estate. It wasn't until she was dying that she told me that he was my father."

"St. Clair!" Eleanor stared at him wide-eyed. "Isn't he the man who. . . ."

"Who gave Bloodstone its name by dying in a pool of blood against those rocks." He nodded and his hand tightened convulsively in hers. "I killed him, Eleanor. I killed my own father." His eyes hardened. "And I would do it again!" He took several deep breaths. "He sent my mother and me away when I was a baby. She had a hard life and died in a cold room with little to show for her life. When she told me, I went to the estate. I found my father outside, in the back. No one saw me. Always been like my mother's people . . . quick and quiet about what I've had to do. If I'd shot Fletcher, he'd never have known it. . . . My father was an old man, almost as old as I am now. I told him who I was and made him promise to come to my mother. I wanted him to give me my rightful name. He promised." His laugh was the sound of rustling leaves. "I waited almost a week. He never came. I would've gone after him, but she was dying. She died one afternoon, and then I went for him. Again he was outside, this time he was near the rocks. I yelled at him and he motioned for me to hold my peace." His tired face paled with the memory.

Eleanor saw the years peel away and his was the face of a young boy not yet a man, filled with loneliness and pain. "Yes?"

"He reached into his pockets and took out money. There was more than two thousand dollars. He told me he had just sold off a piece of the estate to his groundskeeper's son and that the money was for me. . . ." He suddenly beat his fist into the bed. "He was buying me off! He was giving me money instead of my own name! He was giving me money to pay for the life of my mother . . . the years when she scrubbed floors and went hungry!" He looked away. Slowly he turned back to her. The anger and pain was still etched on his face. "We fought. He fell back against the rocks. I didn't even look at him. I just took the money which had fallen to the earth. I walked out vowing that someday I would have everything that should have been mine. Everything! It was a while before I found out I'd killed him. I left the city and then the country. I used his money to make my own."

"Mr. Matthews. . . ." She touched his damp brow.

"There's more. . . . I married an English girl later. We had a girl, but my wife didn't live to see Jane walk. When I could I bought Bloodstone, and summers, when Jane wasn't in a fancy school, we lived on the estate. Jane grew up and hated me for the time we didn't spend together. She was beautiful . . . headstrong . . . she didn't understand. Maybe I didn't know how it was for a girl. . . ." His eyes were bright. "She stayed in England, then came home with a baby in her belly." He looked sharply at the nurse. "Do you know how that was for me? Me, a bastard, cursed by a father who refused me my own name? To see my own child. . . . I did my duty and took care of her. After Michael was born, I wanted to keep him, but she denied me even that. She lived with many men. She drank. She threw my failures in my face, called me a bad father. Maybe I was. I was doing the best I could, but she couldn't see that. Then there was an accident and she was dead, and I had the boy. I wanted to raise him with everything. I wanted to leave him with everything he deserved, everything that was due me, and through me, him. I wanted my land!" His face softened. "Maybe Jane was right. Maybe I was a poor excuse for a father." He looked out the window, peering distantly at the sky. "Now the wheel has turned and I must pay for what I did with a crime I didn't commit. . . ."

He wouldn't say anything more. Eleanor leaned over and kissed his damp forehead. Then she started to leave, tiptoeing, believing he had drifted off to sleep.

"Eleanor?" She turned. "Take care of him for me? And . . . and the child."

Her voice broke with the emotion she felt. "I will, Lucas. But the first way I can help them is to help you. Let me try, please?"

His thin lips curled into a tragic smile. "There is no help . . . . it's my time in the desert. I knew it would come to this. It always must . . . for everyone. . . ."

He was sleeping quietly when she left the room and walked down the long hall to her brother. For the young woman it seemed like a very long walk.

CHAPTER FIFTEEN

THEIR EYES, SO MUCH alike, met each other in anger, locking with unflinching determination.

"You can't do this, Richard! Of all the things you've done in your life nothing has equalled this. He's an old man, and you and I both know he didn't shoot you!" Eleanor folded her arms and glared at him.

The man began to smile. In spite of his bandages and pale complexion he looked relaxed and in relative good spirits. "Can't I? Don't bet on it, sis."

She felt close to tears, and in no way would she give him the satisfaction of seeing her cry. "Please, Richard. You must know who really shot you. Why would you protect the one who did try to kill you? And why would you do this to an old man who's already close to death?"

He shrugged, winced from the sudden pain, and shook his head. His voice dropped to a needling whisper. "Suppose I tell you it was your boyfriend who tried to kill me? Would you like that better?"

She felt a split-second of panic. Then she thought of Michael, and she was calm. She knew it had not been Michael. Her love gave her the vision that even logic lacked. And only then did she remember that Michael had been in his room all that morning and the night before. A peace descended over her and she was glad she'd forgotten the details until she had first felt completely sure that Michael was innocent. "No, I don't believe you. Don't lie to me, Richard. You've lied enough."

His eyes were dark pools of serenity. "You want me to get the old man off the hook?"

She nodded hard.

"Then tell him to sign the paper!"

Michael found her in the hallway. He put his arm around her and led her toward the blue waiting room. "Come on, sweetheart. It'll be okay."

She leaned against him gratefully. "You know?"

He nodded. "Grandfather told me everything. You've been to see your brother?"

She nodded wearily. "He's going to use this to make Lucas sign those papers. Either he really believes that there's a land contractor and he's going to make a lot of money or. . . ." She looked up at Michael. "There's something wrong."

The tall historian nodded and ushered her into the room where Norma, fresh cigarette in her hand, waited. Eleanor glanced at the realtor and let a fresh supply of ideas slip through her mind. *I wonder. . . .*

Michael excused himself to make a phone call. He looked both worried and pleased by the time he returned. The two women had waited quietly for his return, and in the same silence they rode up the mountain and to Bloodstone.

The three of them sat in the library after assuring Mrs. Sanchez that Lucas was well. Norma began to remove papers from her briefcase.

"Now, if you'll just sign here. That will leave room for Lucas' signature, which should appear on the top line."

Eleanor looked up in surprise. "Sign what?"

Norma glanced at her in wide-eyed confusion. "Why, the land contract, of course."

Michael frowned. "Isn't that a little premature, Norma?"

The blonde woman looked at him speculatively, then sighed. "Of course not. I mean, there is no other choice, is there?" She wore an expression of irritation and distaste. "You're certainly not going to let your grandfather rot in some jail, are you?" She held the paper toward him with an impatient gesture.

Eleanor got up. "Michael, don't sign that paper!"

He turned to her. "Well, Norma does have a point, Eleanor. Besides, it's only a formality." He gave her a curious look.

She smiled tightly at Norma Vanowen. "It's been such a difficult day. There's nothing to be done right now, anyway. Would you mind letting Michael think about signing for a day or so, Norma? I wouldn't want him to do anything he might regret." She kept her voice syrup-sweet.

The blonde stood up and angrily began to stuff the papers back in her briefcase. "As you wish. I'm only trying to help." She bit each word off cleanly before going on to the next. When everything was away she walked over to Michael. "Call me when you feel you're ready. I know *you* won't let anything happen to Lucas." She glanced significantly at Eleanor, then looked back at the dark-haired man. "You certainly don't want to risk anything else happening." She began to walk to the door. "But of course, I'm only trying to help." She smiled, showing the perfect teeth. "I can let myself out."

Before Michael could put his expression of confusion into a direct question, Eleanor excused herself to check the baby.

Kierra was overjoyed to awaken from her nap with Eleanor standing over her crib. For a delicious hour the nurse buried herself in the familiar ritual of feeding, bathing, and dressing the baby, and while the infant rocked back on all fours and attempted to crawl, Eleanor sat cross-legged on the floor and began to crochet a doll. All the while she waited. *It feels like it's in the air . . . drifting closer and closer. . . .*

She was giving Kierra her vitamins when she heard the scream from below. "Fire! Fire!" The voice belonged to Teresa Sanchez and from the hallway she heard Ricardo talking excitedly into the telephone. Michael's footsteps thundered down the stairs and out toward the library. She picked up the baby and ran to the door. *At last!* She knew it was this she had been awaiting. . . .

By the time Eleanor reached the library the fire was out and Michael, white shirt streaked with ashes and smoke, was using the fire extinguisher on a last patch of smoking carpet.

"We must leave this place! We must go before more happens!" Teresa Sanchez' voice was tinged with hysteria. She huddled over the ruins of the couch and the desk. "Please! Before more happens here to bring grief to us all."

"That's what someone wants us to do, Mrs. Sanchez." Eleanor started to take the older woman in her arms.

"How dare you touch me!" A shrill scream pierced the silence. It was followed by another, higher yet, and moving closer. From beyond Eleanor could hear the distant wail of a police car or fire truck.

Ricardo pushed Norma into the ruined library, his mouth set in an angry white line.

"Keep your hands off me or I'll have you. . . ." The blonde pulled away from his grip, her face dirty and red with fury. For once her hair was mussed. Little gold tendrils hung damply around her hairline.

Ricardo didn't look at her. He turned to Michael. "I saw her behind the trees. I found this by her." He held out a small gas can.

"It's a lie! I had nothing to do with the fire!" Norma ran the back of her hand across her forehead. She looked up at Michael with a girlish pout. "Michael, make him leave me alone. You know I didn't do anything wrong."

Eleanor noticed that her hand was shaking.

Michael put down the fire extinguisher and looked at Norma. "Why? Why did you do this?" His voice was gentle. She looked away.

Mrs. Sanchez hurried to answer the sharp knocking at the front door. She returned followed by Bill Loenhorst, the sheriff, his deputy, and four members of the volunteer fire department.

Quickly Michael related the events of the afternoon and after a quick inspection, the fire department left. Then he told the sheriff about Norma and the gas can. His voice free of emotion, he speculated about Norma's possible reasons for attempting to set fire to Bloodstone. He looked at her directly for the first time since she had come into the room. "For some reason you want us to sign away this house. I can't believe it's for our own purposes. But I don't understand what it is you hope to get out of it."

The blonde realtor pointedly looked at her nails. "This might shed some light, Dr. Matthews." Loenhorst stepped closer and lowered his voice. He glanced at the blonde. "Jason Reed just paid me a call."

It took Eleanor a moment to place the gatekeeper's son and past owner of the saloon land. "I thought he died!"

At the name Norma froze.

The sheriff turned to Michael. "He was in the hospital for a long time and he has to go back today. He came in to confess shooting Ken Fletcher." He paused to let his words sink in. "It seems Fletcher and Miss Vanowen were in cahoots on some land swindle and got Reed to sign away his land to them," he said in his easy drawl. "Old Jason didn't even realize what had happened until two weeks ago, and when he confronted Fletcher, he got laughed off his own property. Seems he made more than one attempt to kill him. So your grandfather's in the clear." He looked at Norma Vanowen. "I guess you and Fletcher were closer than any of us suspected." He smiled a crooked grin. "My youngest boy told me he saw you and Fletcher together in his car one night up by the campgrounds." He gestured toward his deputy. "How about escorting the lady down the hill? She's got some explaining to do."

As the deputy took her arm, Norma turned back to Michael. "You really believed that the contractor was just for appearances, didn't you? Do you have any idea how much I stood to make?" She looked scornfully at the nurse by his side. "But you had to listen to her. It would have been so simple."

Eleanor watched Norma, her head thrown back proudly, stride out of the room, the deputy close at her heels.

The sheriff started to follow and then stopped. "Almost forgot," he said, snapping his fingers. "I checked into that Robert St. Clair death you asked me to look up."

Eleanor held the baby a little closer and looked at Michael in surprise.

"Yes?" Michael's voice was suddenly tense.

He shrugged. "Seems the old man died of a massive coronary, not from what was a very superficial wound on the head. The case was closed a long time ago. It was his third and final heart attack. I don't see any point in involving ourselves with the matter at all after this much time." He tipped his hat and left the room.

CHAPTER SIXTEEN

THE BABY SCREWED her face into a comical yawn before dropping off to sleep. Her little body stretched out comfortably and a drop of milk glazed her lower lip. Her tiny fingers, like graceful pink fish, curled around the satin edge of her blanket.

Eleanor put the yellow duck next to her gently. "Sleep, good girl. It's been a long day."

Michael touched a blonde curl tenderly. "A very long day." His dark eyes stayed on the baby's sweet face. They were soft and loving. "Eleanor, she's really beautiful . . . very, very beautiful. I want to spend some time with her tomorrow. I want to get to know her." He turned to the young woman and took her hand.

"That would be nice," she said softly. But inside she felt a twinge of disappointment. She had known it would be like this once he knew that Kierra was his daughter. *I suppose it's for the best. However it comes out in the end! . . .*

Michael kissed her gently. "I've done a great deal of thinking about something I asked you once . . . about what it takes to be a father. I've decided the biology doesn't matter." He looked at her earnestly. "It just doesn't matter. Not to me. Not anymore, if it ever did. I just want to learn to be a father to her."

She looked up at him, a frown wrinkling her forehead. "I . . . didn't your grandfather tell you? About Ken, my brother?"

"What do you mean?"

She could see that his grandfather had left it up to her. She told him immediately, a great joy filling her soul.

He went back to the crib and stared down at his daughter. "I'm glad you waited to tell me. This way I'll always know I love her for herself, and not because she's my flesh and blood." He turned and took her in his arms. "You know, I was afraid to ask you to marry me, Eleanor. I thought that if Kierra was mine, there might be something wrong with her. But all she needed was love. And that's what we're going to give all of our children."

"I think Lucas will like that." She smiled against his shoulder.

"He'll have that and his land, too. I think Jason's ready to sell now." He looked at her. "But I think the children will have more to do with restoring Bloodstone more meaningfully than a little more property." He kissed her.

From the crib came the soft gurgling of a happy, sleeping baby.